MW01231414

TABLE OF CONTENTS

INTRODUCTION

All of the narratives and characters in this book of short stories are fictionalized. However, some of the actual climactic events are true and have transpired in the lives of people I have once encountered who have confided in me, they shall remain nameless.

The title, *"Twisted Tells"* is a double entendre that came about due to the tales being twisted in nature - as in abnormal, unhealthy and disturbing; as well as twisted - as in completely altered.

The stories that are not of truthful culminating events were me allowing my imagination to run amok.

"BEST FRIENDS"
(CHAPTER 1)

He was the one everyone liked. He made excellent grades in school- was handsome and very sociable. He also was very generous, didn't have much, but what he did have he was more than willing to share. If one of his friends did not have enough money for lunch, he would gladly give them half of his. If one of his friends spent the night at his house, he would let them wear his clothes if they saw something of his they liked, and would help anyone with their homework if they were struggling. This was how he was in elementary, middle and high school. The teachers and students alike loved him. There was only one problem; he was reared in a household that was far from financially secure, which came with an accompanying neighborhood that was a breeding ground for various criminal activity.

His parents were still together, struggled financially their entire lives, but made the best life they could for him with what they had. They instilled priceless values in him although they had very little to offer him monetarily, however, there was a roof over his head, food to eat and a jalopy they helped him purchase to get back and forth to wherever he needed to go when he entered high school.

Nevertheless, these values were manifested in his loyalty, thoughtfulness, selflessness, as well as giving his all in school. There was one of the guys from the neighborhood who he became the closest with. His name was Leon. Leon was reared by a single mother, his father was not around and his mother allowed him to come and go as he pleased while in high school. Leon chose to spend most of his time at Brandon's house since his parents loved him like he was their own son, fed him, and allowed him to ride along with the family to run errands or go to the park with them for their family cookouts on holidays or other special occasions.

Leon was the brother Brandon always wanted, but never had since he was an only child. Brandon admired Leon for being able to come and go as he pleased, something his parents did not allow; but Leon admired Brandon for having both of his parents still together, the love they had for him and the time they spent with him - something he did not have.

In high school people who did not know them actually thought they were related because they were so close. Eventually, they became very popular because they would come to school dressed nice from head to toe every single day and had a vehicle - despite it being a hooptie, while other students were riding the school bus, most notably referred to as "the cheese". Sometimes Brandon would even let Leon drive while he relaxed in the passenger seat.

Brandon worked at a retail store since the 9th grade, saved his money to buy the things he wanted and shared them as he always did with everyone else, especially with his best friend Leon. His parents were very proud of the man he was becoming and felt they owed it to him to let him do what he wanted with his earnings since he never had much prior to obtaining a job. They just told him to not spend it all on insignificant material things and try to save some of it for a rainy day.

Brandon and Leon both eventually graduated high school and had more time on their hands. Neither of them ever thought about going to college since their parents could not afford it, nor did anyone in their families go past having a high school education. The thought also never crossed their minds to open a business since the only entrepreneur they ever knew was Pee Wee, who did well, but in their eyes, because he did not have a flashy lifestyle, did not earn enough to impress the 2 young men to want to follow in his footsteps, so neither direction was even on their radar. They were both from generations of poverty. Brandon was lucky to land the retail job in the 9th grade that the neighborhood clothing store owner Pee Wee gave him because he loved his sociable personality and felt he would be a great fit for that line of work, but his buddy Leon was never employed.

Brandon had a loyal customer who had been coming into the clothing store every month for years to purchase new attire and would often talk to him about the next trip he was taking out of state, the next concert he was getting tickets for, a nice restaurant he was taking his girlfriend to and the next vehicle purchase he was contemplating. He would also leave Brandon a nice tip when he helped him in the store.

Brandon was impressed by this although he was able to buy nice clothes since the 9th grade due to having the retail job that also came with a generous discount and had the ability to save up and help purchase his 1st used car while in high school since he had been working, but this was a completely different level, it was a lifestyle he had never had the opportunity to experience since his parents were financially unable to expose him to vacations, concerts, various restaurants or brand new cars.

Although the guy had been coming into the store for the past few years and they often engaged in small talk, Brandon finally got up the courage to ask him what he did for a living. The guy responded, "How about I just show you." Brandon was elated that his longtime customer that he built a rapport with over the years and was always impressed with was willing to take him under his wing. The guy who called himself "Ace" told Brandon he would pick him up after he get off work later that evening. Brandon told Ace he was closing the store tonight and his shift should be over at about 10:00 pm. Ace told him he would pick him up at that time.

Closing time finally arrived and Ace kept his word. He was there to pick up Brandon in his shiny late model sports car that Brandon really adored at 10:00 sharp. Ace took Brandon to grab a bite to eat and off they went. He went to 3 different locations to introduce Brandon to the only 3 guys in the city he trusted and did business with.

They all drove nice automobiles, had beautiful homes, expensive jewelry and stylish clothes. Brandon wanted to be a part of that circle so badly. They treated him like a younger brother since Ace introduced him and they all trusted and highly respected Ace.

After leaving, Ace told Brandon that he was a "street pharmacist" and those were the guys who distributed for him. He told Brandon he would allow him to hang out with him a few more times and he can decide if he wanted to keep selling all of the retail clothing to others while only getting a few outfits here and there or be the one purchasing them whenever he wanted and actually having somewhere to wear them to on a regular basis. Brandon opted for the latter.

Before long, Ace had Brandon doing his deals after work and when the money began rolling in in large sums, he resigned from the retail store he had worked in since high school. Pee-Wee, the thin old man who owned the retail store tried to tell Brandon that Ace is not the type of guy he want to get mixed up with outside of selling him clothes and shoes. Brandon respected and loved Pee Wee like an uncle, but had a strong desire to live this new lifestyle, which led to the store owner having to hire someone else.

Ace begin to trust Brandon so much because of how good he was doing and how he always kept his word, he eventually allowed him to handle larger and larger amounts of his product. He fit right in with the 3 guys Ace initially introduced him to. He eventually purchased a nice new car, jewelry, fine clothing, was taking trips out of town, dining at various restaurants and finally got his first place - a nice luxurious high rise river front apartment downtown.

Leon finally caught up with Brandon, since they had not had much time to really talk in a while, and told him he knew he was not getting all of his new items from just that retail job. Brandon admitted to his best friend that he quit the retail job and had been working for Ace, but had not got around to telling him yet.

Brandon was skeptical about mentioning it to his best friend since Ace schooled him on how to always move in silence by not letting anyone know the moves he was making unless they were part of the small circle who was moving the weight, how not to wear expensive clothes and jewelry around people who can't afford the same thing, how to continue to drive his old car when riding around the hood and only to pull the new car out when he was going out of town or somewhere nice in order to not be a target. However, Brandon did not feel comfortable keeping secrets from his best friend since they grew up together, were so close, and he felt he can trust him to not tell anyone.

Leon immediately knew who Ace was because he was a well-known street guy who had been dealing in large amounts of product for years and rumor had it that he had a solid plug straight out of Columbia. Leon said he heard some of the guys in his neighborhood talking about him often and although he tries to be low-key, the streets talk and people know he's making major moves.

Leon and Brandon remained friends after all of these years when many of their other peers went their separate ways - although Brandon was not spending as much time with Leon as he used to. Brandon allowed Leon to drive his older car sometimes when he drove the newer one he purchased and when they would go out of town or somewhere nice around the city together, he would get in the passenger seat and let Leon drive the new car, just as he did in high school. He would also take Leon shopping with him whenever he went to the mall. He continued to treat him like the brother he never had. Brandon had all of the girls wanting to go out with him and Leon was able to ride his coattail; however, although he did not admit it, Leon was slightly jealous despite Brandon sharing everything with him.

Eventually, Leon asked Brandon if he could introduce him to Ace so he can have direct access to the type of money he was getting. Brandon told Leon he would definitely run it by Ace and see what he says. When Brandon approached Ace about it, he was told no, he could not help his friend out since he did not know him personally, and that he only deal with people he has known for many years and know directly not indirectly through someone else.

Brandon was slightly offended since he thought his word of saying Leon was a trustworthy guy who he grew up with and was best friends with would stand for something. Ace went on explaining to Brandon, "That's how people get caught up - trying to let people in they don't know based on someone else's word". Ace told Brandon to watch the movie "Donnie Brasco", which was based on a true story, and he would understand.

When he brought the news to Leon, he felt bitter about it and asked Brandon if he told Ace how they have been friends since elementary school. Brandon told him he mentioned all of that, but Ace was still skeptical because he only let people in that he personally grew up with or had a direct connection with for years in some type of way.

Brandon explained to Leon how Ace went on saying that's how people get caught up and the movie he told him to watch. Leon then asked Brandon if he could just work for him with the product he was getting from Ace instead. Brandon stated he did not want to break Ace's trust or lose his respect by secretly going against him. Leon told Brandon Ace would never find out; Brandon stood firm and told Leon he was not willing to take that type of risk with Ace's product and reminded Leon how he always take him shopping with him, let him drive his car, give him pocket money when he needs it, etc. Leon angrily replied to Brandon, "Man that's not the same as having your own!" Brandon promised Leon if he ever gets his own connection he would put him on. Leon responded with a dissatisfied, "Alright man".

Brandon suggested to Leon that he apply for a job at one of the plants since they paid well and told him in the meantime he would put a good word in with old man Pee Wee at the retail shop for him. Leon looked at Brandon with the side eye and stated how he is not trying to be on nobody's job for 8 hours a day when he can work for himself and how he is not trying to work at a retail shop for minimum wage when he can make at least a few thousand dollars a week even in a slow month selling weight. Brandon reminded him how he did it for over 5 years. Leon said, "That's different, you worked there mostly while we were in high school, and we're grown men now". Brandon eventually dropped the subject to avoid any more friction with his friend.

Nevertheless, life goes on and Leon and Brandon continued to be friends, but deep inside Leon wanted to be just like Brandon and eventually started feeling distant since he was no longer the one Brandon spent all of his time with, and felt pushed aside since Ace did not trust him coming into the circle. Although Brandon had no control of his boss's decision, Leon still had misplaced animosity towards Brandon.

One night, Brandon and Leon were in Brandon's new convertible and Brandon was about to drop Leon off after a long fun late night of partying. Leon was commenting to Brandon how, "They were all on you man", speaking of the attractive ladies at the party. Leon was secretly seething and had been for several months now seeing how Brandon was becoming well known as the handsome, nice, giving guy who was doing well for himself and how he was just the friend of the guy with all the nice things, which only got him so far.

Leon asked Brandon to make a stop before he went home. Brandon thought nothing of it and told him sure. They stopped in the parking lot of a closed store; Brandon asked Leon, "Why are we stopping here?" Leon stated he wanted to talk to him about something. As Brandon begin to let the convertible top up while they were parked in the dark empty parking lot - 2 men in ski masks came running from behind the store and made it to the car before the top closed. One of them put a thick clear plastic bag over Brandon's head.

He begin to fight them off as best he could while unable to breathe, his eyes were dilated as he looked horrified, confused, and tried to reach for his gun in the armrest, which he did not have a chance to get to. He realized Leon was in on it as he offered no help while he was fighting for his life. After the guys beat and suffocated

Brandon, they went through his pockets, took off his jewelry, left his body in the parking lot, jumped into his car, then sped off fishtailing and burning rubber.

The next morning, a store employee found Brandon's body in the empty lot. Leon was called to the police station since he was reported to be the last one to see him alive after they left the party together the night before. He made a statement of how he was dropped off by Brandon after the party and did not hear from him since. The Detectives had no other evidence to go and had to allow Leon to walk out of the precinct.

The funeral was eventually held, Leon attended it as if nothing happened and even spoke at the podium about their closeness, years of friendship and how he loved him like a brother. Several weeks went past, Leon's DNA was found in the car and on the body, which was to be expected since he was with him the night of his death and was often in the car with him. 2 other unidentified male DNA specimens were also discovered. Several months then went past, Leon checked in with Brandon's family periodically and they appreciated it since they always looked at him as their other son.

Meanwhile, the detectives were still on the case trying to figure out who killed Brandon. Since there were no witnesses and the store's cameras were non-functional, they had to wait until they got a hit from the national database to see who the other DNA specimens belonged to, which could take years depending on if the other 2 men get caught committing another crime that required the collection of their DNA or if there was a long shot one of the men would feel compelled to come forward and confess.

Several months turned into several years, Ace could not stop thinking about the murder of Brandon, the young man he took under his wing. One day he and the only 3 guys he truly trusted were talking about what transpired that night and Ace had an epiphany. He thought back to the day Brandon came to him asking if Leon could join the crew and he turned the idea down. Ace never asked then, but now wondered how Leon felt about the rejection.

Ace and his 3 close friends & business partners wondered if there was a possibility that Leon felt jilted and jealous enough to rob and kill his best friend. Since Ace knew enough about Leon through stories Brandon used to tell him, he decided he would use that knowledge to see if he could get more information.

Ace had a couple of female friends he truly trusted, had known for years and who would do anything for him. He sent one of them to Leon's neighborhood where he knew he would be hanging outside with other guys as Brandon said he always did until he went by to pick him up to go somewhere with him.

The plan worked like a charm. The young lady parked outside the corner store Leon was known to frequent until she saw who appeared to be him go in, she quickly got out of her car and of course she was a new cute face and all of the guys were trying to talk to her. She acted interested in Leon after she confirmed which one he was when one of his friends called his name, and he fell for the bait. They exchanged numbers, she would go by and pick him up, and with the money Ace gave her - pay when they went out to eat when he was unable to and even became intimate with him to get close enough to be able to talk to him about anything and everything just as Ace instructed her to do.

Shannon and Leon would have fun together and talk a lot. After a few months she finally thought the time was right to indirectly ask about Brandon. She eased it in to test the temperature of how he would respond. She lied and said that her cousin was killed in a car accident about 5 years ago, which she blames herself for since she was driving, only sustained minor injuries and how they were so close they called each other sisters and how she could not stop thinking about her even though it happened a while back.

She asked him if he had ever lost anyone close to him. Leon hesitated at first, but then begin to open up and tell her how he was really close with a guy he knew since elementary school, but how he felt he betrayed him after they graduated high school by not putting him on with his connection that would've gave him access to making a lot of money and thinking free outfits, being treated to lunch or dinner, and letting him drive his old car was supposed to be enough. Leon went on to say he was killed in a robbery after being beat and suffocated with a plastic bag over his head, but stated he didn't feel sorry for him because of how they were supposed to be brothers, but he left him behind.

Shannon went back to tell Ace about the conversation. Ace then said, "No one ever said he was suffocated or had a plastic bag put over his head, they only said he was beat to death." He figured if this were true, Leon had to know more than he told the Detectives based on their statements to the media.

Ace had Shannon make an anonymous call to the precinct to mention the conversation she had with Leon. When they tried to ask her for more identifying information, she just hung up the phone, but they had enough to know she was on to something since they had never released that piece of information to the public or to family about Brandon being suffocated with a bag over his head. They purposely let on as if he was only beat to death.

Detectives and Officers immediately went to Leon's house, where he still lived with his mother with a search warrant and an arrest warrant. They put Leon in handcuffs and packed up almost everything in his bedroom, then took it out in boxes and brown paper bags. The lab meticulously combed through the clothes, shoes, jewelry and other items while Leon was in the Interrogation Room. The Detective asked Leon how did his best friend die? Leon loudly responded, "You already questioned me about this man, I told you, I know what everybody else know, he was beat and suffocated with a plastic bag over his head!"

The Detective then asked him how did he find out about Brandon being suffocated since it wasn't in the news? He said Brandon's parents told him. The Detective told Leon to come again because that information was never released to anyone, not even Brandon's parents. Leon then told the Detective he wanted an Attorney.

The Lab Technician phoned the Detective to inform him that Leon's watch had dried blood in between the crevices of the links. Leon was immediately officially booked for probable cause of murder. While Leon sat in jail since he was unable to post bail, a case was building against him. The blood testing returned a few weeks later and it was positive for Brandon's DNA. Leon was unable to explain how Brandon's blood was in the crevices of his watch when Brandon was not bleeding when they left the party and if he said he was dropped off after the party never to see Brandon again, why did he fail to mention any injury Brandon sustained that would have caused him to bleed.

The Detective called Brandon's parents to inform them that they have one of Brandon's killers. The parents asked who it was and was told Leon Payne. They were in disbelief, they asked the detectives if they were sure and assured them Leon would not be involved in such a thing. The Detective informed Brandon's parents, Mr. and Mrs. Commons that Leon knew a detail they purposefully left out to ensure they had the killer or someone who knew the killers if that piece of information was ever mentioned.

Brandon's parents were hit with a triple whammy after learning their son's best friend was one of the murderers, he was suffocated with a plastic bag over his head on top of being beaten to death, and after learning the watch that blood was found in between the links of was the nice timepiece Brandon purchased for Leon as a just because gift.

The District Attorney offered Leon a deal after okaying it with Brandon's parents of shaving off 10 years of his 30 year sentence he was seeking if he gave up the other 2 unidentified men involved. Leon sang like a nightingale and the other 2 men were brought to justice after a thorough investigation.

The parents figured that was a small price to pay to ensure all involved were punished for killing their beloved son, and Ace felt a weight lifted off his chest by knowing he helped Brandon postmortem, since he felt partially responsible for introducing him to the fast flashy lifestyle that caused him to be a magnet for as it turns out, robbery and death. He also felt he went about it in the best way to avoid any heat or interference with his street enterprise that he had plans on flipping into a legit business.

Words of Wisdom: It is never worth it to choose the path of a dangerous lifestyle no matter how fun and fabulous it seems. It is highly likely that it will be short lived and be met with dire consequences.

"BLINDED"
(CHAPTER 2)

He came from an outstanding 4 family household and had an envious upbringing to most. His father was a Professor at the local University, and his mother worked as Lead Faculty at a nearby State College. It was how they met decades earlier, after attending the Annual Educator's Convention. They eventually married and had 2 boys, Travis and Tobias.

The eldest son, Travis was now 19 and did not spend much

time with his younger brother since they were 5 years apart. They both had their own set of friends. Travis graduated high school, but did not have the desire to attend college, go into the military or work a full time job as his parents encouraged. He would say to them, "I'm not going to school for all of those years and end up making less than 6 figures or slaving on someone else's job making them rich, and I'm definitely not trying to go to war and kill people who haven't done anything to me."

His parents would try to reason with him that it's about studying something he would love to do, finding a job that would bring him a decent steady income or simply working to save enough money in order to open his own business one day, which either way will be beneficial over the years. Travis then responded, "That's gonna take too long".

He was not trying to hear that, he eventually moved out of the family home since he was given an ultimatum by his parents to enroll in school somewhere, find a job or he would have to leave. His parents told him they were no longer going to provide for him if he was not going to do something productive with his life.

Travis ended up living with 3 other guys, one who

happened to be his cousin. They were all street hustlers. His cousin was a few years older, grew up across town and came from a totally different upbringing. This lifestyle seemed to appeal to Travis more than the one he was brought up in. The guys showed him the ropes and before long, he began selling stolen electronics, boosting clothes, credit card scams, as well as dealing marijuana since he felt if he was ever caught it would not land him a lot of jail time.

This was the good life in Travis' eyes. Although he grew up having family vacations, occasional money for shopping, living in an upper middle class neighborhood and having his parents purchase him a brand new compact car on his 16th birthday, this new way of life was different. He didn't have a clothing budget, nor did he have to drive a compact car anymore or live by anyone else's rules but his own. He was at the mall almost every weekend, purchased a much bigger vehicle, and eventually moved into a nice spacious town house; Travis was living it up and enjoying every minute of it.

When Travis would stop by his parents' home to visit his younger brother Tobias, they would never let the younger brother leave with Travis because they knew there was only one way he was obtaining all of these luxuries, which was illegally since he was not working and they did not want Tobias caught up in that lifestyle.

His father would try to talk to him when he stopped by the house by saying, "Travis, I know it's nice to have all of these things, but they won't last forever if you continue on this path". Travis would just say, "I hear you Dad", and leave since he did not want to hear his parents lecture him.

Travis is enjoying out of town trips, every event he desires to attend, partying, shopping and living like many people only wished they could. This goes on for several years, and one night after leaving his cousin and friends to head back to his town house, Travis makes a quick stop at the gas station. As he was at the pump, 2 gunmen swiftly approach him in dark clothing and face masks robbing him for his jewelry, cash and SUV. They shot Travis right between the eyes and left him for dead before getting away with almost $6,000 in cash, about $10,000 worth of jewelry and taking off in his vehicle, which was later found at a chop shop that was raided.

Someone eventually saw him lying there bleeding and called 911. Attempts of resuscitation were being made while he was being rushed to the nearest hospital. Once he arrived at the emergency room, his pulse was slowly fading; the doctors hooked him up to ventilators, monitors, defibrillators and IV's. His chances of survival were slim. His family was called and spent the night at the hospital waiting to hear something from the medical staff.

Several days passed and the doctor approached the family one morning to inform them that Travis made it through the toughest part and should be OK; there were sighs of relief, hugs and tears of joy. However, the doctor had to inform the family that he would be in a wheelchair for a while, will need to relearn his motor skills, and will never be able to see again due to severe optic nerve damage from the 22 caliber bullet that they had to leave lodged in his head because it was too risky to go in to retrieve it.

The moment was bittersweet. Although the family was saddened by the medical prognosis, they were still elated that Travis survived. His parents took him back home to care for him. Over several months he regained the majority of his motor skills and no longer needed the wheelchair. However, he had to learn to live a new life. His parents purchased him a red and white cane and paid for Braille reading lessons. Travis adapted very well and eventually enrolled into the university that his father taught at. He flourished in school and graduated with a double major. Travis wanted to live the fast life, but it took for him to go blind to be able to see the right path.

Ballers

There are many across the U.S.

Who are balling out of **control**

Some use their own supply

While others know better than

to get high

A portion keeps a low profile

While others ball it out with

style

From wearing the biggest

brand **names**

To sitting at front row **games**

A business they may main**tain**

To justify expensive claims

Definitely for these ballers

Money ain't a thang

Around the **globe** taking trips

And always leave hefty tips

There's only one thing though

They better not slip

Because the **feds** will hunt their

heads

Awaiting a **chance** to im**bed**

So will friends or ene**mies**

Who might get'm instead

Having'm meet destiny

With **caskets** and stone **beds**

Words of Wisdom: More often than not, the slower route is the route that brings longevity.

BLOOD
ON THE
BOULEVARD
(CHAPTER 3)

Joseph was one of the nicest people you would ever want to meet. He never told people no even if it inconvenienced him to assist them with something. He was usually quiet and stayed to himself unless he was at a social event where he would open up a little bit. He also always ignored anyone who would attempt to slight him. Some would even describe him as meek. Nevertheless, he was a hardworking man who never bothered anyone.

He often told stories of his past and how he was bullied a lot in school due to his extremely quiet nature. Joseph stated the kids at school would call him mute, a wus, and even ask him if he was deaf and dumb. He would just ignore them and continue playing alone as he preferred to do.

Growing up as an only child, Joseph was fine with playing by himself and using his imagination, a behavior that caused him to be very creative, but more of a loner even in adulthood. He was always exceptionally shy, but the extreme shyness had begun to more and more impede on his social development; it caused him to become an outcast, have low self-esteem, feel lonely, and he even showed signs of Depression. However, he tried to become more sociable by going to a few work events, but he would still find himself not as involved as he preferred to be.

This transferred into his dating life. Joseph would see a girl he admired and wanted to get to know better, but would always be too nervous to say anything. He would just stare at her, and when she looked over he would sheepishly turn his head away feeling embarrassed that he was caught watching her. Of course, this got him nowhere with the ladies; Joseph was now 40 years old, had never been married, never had children and pretty much never had an actual relationship. His only socialization with women was co-workers and friends of the family. Everyone realized that he was socially awkward and usually kept a distance, not realizing this exacerbated the situation. However, he did have more communication and socialization skills with his family, but it never ventured out further than those relatives.

Joseph was really bothered and dejected about this and even went to see a therapist. She had him complete homework assignments to help open him up more and they even delved deep into his history to see if there was anything there that could be causing the problem. There was no childhood trauma or abuse; it was just extreme shyness that he never broke out of that became worse over the years. She diagnosed him with Severe Anxiety Disorder and prescribed him medication. Joseph reported to his therapist that the medication made him feel drowsy and numb, so he ceased taking it.

Eventually, Joseph became worse; he felt there was no hope since his therapist could not help him feel better as he thought she should have been able to do. His coworkers did not make the situation better by keeping their distance, and his family he felt treated him like they felt sorry for him, which Joseph despised. His mother would make suggestions of things for him to do, but he felt at 40, as much as he loved his mother and as much as he knew she was only trying to help, he should not be following her direction for his social and dating life.

Today was the day. Joseph had convinced himself that his quality of life was descending and he saw no improvement in sight. He decided there was no point of being among the living if he would always feel completely emotionally and socially disconnected. Joseph purchased a hotel room on the top floor with a beautiful balcony view over the city for the evening, kept the sliding glass door open for the fresh breeze that was coming through, watched a few of his favorite television shows and called his mother to tell her he loved her and that he would see her soon.

He then went to the far end of his hotel room and ran as fast as he could until he jumped straight off of the balcony. He fell from the 19th floor to his death, which landed him on the street in front of the hotel called "The Boulevard". When Joseph told his mother he would see her soon, little did she know at the time, he meant when they meet up in the afterlife.

Words to Remember: There is a wise quote that states, "Suicide is a permanent solution to a temporary problem".

All problems are temporary since one can always find ways to make them easier to deal with or even use the energy to channel into something productive.

Joseph could have found solace in attending support groups with other people facing the same issues, that way he would have known he was not alone, would have had people he could relate to and could have saw there was hope in his situation. In a support group, he would have heard a myriad of ways to deal with his issue from others who have already been through it or were currently going through it, he would have heard from speakers who overcame similar issues, and he would have had a group of people he would have more easily opened up to, networked with and built supportive relationships and understanding with since they were all a reflection of the same issue that caused his struggle that eventually lead to his demise.

Words of Wisdom: There is always help, if one way does not work, keep trying until you find what does. Everything will never work for everyone; you have to find what works for you.

BURN BABY BURN!!
(CHAPTER 4)

She grew up in a low income, high risk home and neighborhood. Her mother was unable to rear her properly due to her drug addiction and was never home because she was too busy running the streets all times of the night and chasing her high, which left her in the home to fend for herself as a young child. She never even knew who her father was. This led to her going hungry many days, being frightened most nights due to being home alone, not going to school and barely having a bath because her mother rarely paid the bills leaving no hot water in the home. Eventually, child protective services were called and little Sandy was sent to foster care.

After residing in foster care for 2 years, her maternal grandmother was able to bring her home and take care of her. Her grandmother tried her best to rear her correctly, but it was difficult with not knowing who the child's father was to obtain financial support from, no decent male or female role models outside of herself, the child having a mother strung out on drugs and them having to reside in an area where there was an abundance of drug dealing, alcohol and drug use, as well as violence and crime. The outside influence took over throughout the years and Sandy eventually repeated her mother's mistakes, habits, and lifestyle despite her grandmother's best efforts.

She eventually became pregnant several times, resulting in most of her children testing positive for illegal drugs after birth and ultimately having to be taken from her custody, just as she was from her mother. After a number of years, Sandy eventually decided to get the help she needed to obtain custody of her 4 children back from the state. Her grandmother was too elderly and frail by now to raise young children, and although she attempted to get Sandy's kids for her too, the courts would not allow it.

Sandy relapsed half way through the drug rehabilitation program she was enrolled in after having strong urges to use again and leaving the program unsuccessfully to go and get high. She was so disappointed in herself she locked herself in the bedroom where she still had a place to stay with her grandmother for days.

After crying for countless hours from the anguish of repeating her mother's mistakes, having thoughts of losing her children to her drug addiction, not being able to find decent employment, and seeing herself as worthless, she decided she should be punished and needed physical pain to take away from the mental pain.

Sandy decided she would not be a cutter; she preferred to be a burner. Sandy doused herself in flammable fluid and lit her cigarette lighter. As she began to scream from the pain of the flames and held on to the headboard of her bed to forcefully attempt to take the pain of the fire melting her skin and burning her hair, her grandmother ran into the room after hearing her screams - saw her on fire, beat the flames off of her with a nearby pillow then called 911 to report the emergency! As her grandmother tried to caress and console her after the flames were gone, she had to cease when Sandy's skin begin peeling off from the burns.

After being admitted and treated at the hospital's burn unit, Sandy recovered despite being scarred for life with obvious burns over half of her body. She reported to the medical staff that the flammable liquid spilled in her bed because it was leaking from a shopping bag without her knowledge after she tried to light her cigarette and her bed burst into flames while she was sitting on it. However, once Sandy got home after months in the hospital into her grandmother's loving arms, she admitted to her that she attempted to burn herself to death to self-avenge the neglect and abuse she allowed her children to endure in foster care and living house to house while she was in the streets drinking and drugging all of these years. She admitted that she did not feel she should go on living since she was unable to do right for herself or her children by staying sober.

More years pass by of Sandy working on bettering herself after this incident. She initiated custody of her 2 youngest children with the state's child protective services since the first 2 were now young adults. She completed the rehabilitation program, frequented a psychiatrist that was paid for by the state, accomplished getting her GED, obtained a job, and eventually acquired her own residence and transportation. She successfully obtained full custody of her 2 younger children after supervised then unsupervised visits. She was able to make amends with her

2 young adult children who forgave her and helped out with their 2 younger siblings.

Sandy also revealed to all of the children that the burn scars were intentional and not accidental as they had thought all of these years. She explained to the children why she did it and how she did it. They all hugged and cried together and vowed to always be there for each other. Sandy educated all of her children on how to stay in positive environments, around positive people, to always progress and better themselves, how to stay busy with constructive occupations and recreational activities and protect themselves to avoid having diseases or children they are not ready for or able to care for.

Although Sandy walked around for the rest of her life with severe burn scars over half of her body including her face and neck, and always received stares and whispers from strangers, she did not care about what others said or thought because as Sandy put it, "My mental and emotional pain was more excruciating than this burn injury and these external scars can never compare to my internal scarring. I would rather have these burn scars to remind me of the pain I once endured and overcame due to my past lifestyle than to walk around unscarred externally, but still scarred internally". It was years in the making, but Sandy was a changed woman and often went back to the rehabilitation program she was once in to tell her story to other addicts in recovery. There was never a dry eye in the building when she was done speaking.

Self-injury- The act of harming yourself, it's usually not meant as a suicide attempt, rather a harmful way to cope with emotional pain, intense anger and frustration. (mayoclinic.org, 2018) However, Sandy took hers further, her mission was to complete suicide, until her grandmother walked into the room and saved her life.

FREAKS OF NATURE

When one disrupts the natural flow of nature, her wrath will be felt!

(CHAPTER 5)

There's a rare zoological museum that sits in Michigan, right off the Detroit River. It is beautifully architecturally structured and its interior is as rare as its exterior. The window panes have colorful distinctive images of animals that are found in various countries all over the world, many of which are collected and housed inside for exhibition in numerous forms such as skeletal, taxidermy, fluid preserved, and some even living.

Thousands of tourists enter the doors annually to get a glimpse of the rarely and some even never before seen unusual creatures. Ezel, the museum's Zoologist and Chief Explorer and his team travel to the peaks of the highest mountains, the bottom of the lowest valleys, the deepest of the darkest caves, the most extreme of bitter wintry freezing cold and scorching hot climates in search of rare animal life to bring back to the zoological museum for display, as well as collect some of the surrounding habitation to replicate the environment.

Ezels's next journey has taken him to the thick, daring but dazzling jungles of Africa. Ezel is sure he will find a rare creature in the African brush if he goes in deeper than no other has gone before. As he is dropped off in the middle of the jungle by a small aircraft and pilot funded by the museum, he navigates through the tropical jungle bypassing different creatures that have already been identified seeking a rare find.

He begins to trek further into the thick green jungle, camping out in camouflage with his camping backpack filled with just the essentials needed to get him by for the next few weeks he is prepared to spend there if necessary. As night falls, he lightly sleeps and patiently awaits the break of dawn each day to continue his journey until he can discover something he can photograph and take back in order to bring a team with him to later capture, or for a find he can capture himself with the apparatus he keeps in his backpack.

Ezel's patience pays off! He comes across his first glimpse of an unidentified species. It looks to be an enormous bird, but upon further observation, as he creeps cautiously closer peering through his binoculars, it turns out to be a monkey with wings spanning 20 feet wide flying limb to limb throughout the massive jungle trees! Ezel's eyes open as wide as the sky; he is frozen solid in disbelief, shock, and fear at what he identifies as a winged monkey! Ezel was prepared to find a rare species, but not an impossible creature! He runs as fast as his legs will carry him, tripping several times along the way until he gets to the designated lift off spot where he radioed his pilot to meet him. As they fly out of the jungle, the pilot drops him off below as instructed.

Ezel finds his way to the nearest remote village by following the voices and sounds of human life he hears, he then comes across native village people who do not live far from the jungle. They have frequently heard of him and his finds and mostly thought he was psychotic for going so deep into the jungle; they also believed most of it was all a hoax that he and the museum curators were manipulating and conspiring to fool people in order to turn a profit and build a reputation for themselves and their museum.

He frantically describes the species he has just witnessed to this small group of villagers he saw gathered nearby in the best version of their native dialect that he could speak. They express amusement, but laugh in disbelief telling him how foolish he sounds. Ezel then catches a ride in a rusty muddy jeep passing by to the scientific college lab he had visited a few times before, which sat in a small town several miles away from the outskirts of the jungle to inquire about the biological possibility of what he witnessed.

The Professor and Lead Scientist, Dr. Sycamore explains to Ezel condescendingly how humans and animals are more alike than they are different and if some humans have the desire to mate outside of their race and gender, why can't some animals do so outside of their species? Dr.

Sycamore shared "top secret" research with Ezel since he was a fellow colleague in the professional science field that detailed how the animal kingdom has been witnessed by very few mating with opposite species; and how it's so uncommon, that the scientific community and society as a whole would never accept it without proof. He then cited what he considered the "perfect examples" of how the mule is the offspring of a male donkey and female horse, as well as the liger being the offspring of a male lion and female tiger. Dr. Sycamore went on saying how it was bound to happen with other species sooner or later and how he does not understand why he's so baffled and amused by it.

Before leaving the college laboratory, Ezel asked Dr. Sycamore if he could work with him to capture and study the unidentified mutant. Ezel was astounded when the scientist with the genius research reputation of being one of the best in the world would decline such an offer to join him for the study of an unfamiliar creature that could possibly catapult both of their careers and the sciences even further, but thought no more of the declined collaboration. Nevertheless, Ezel left the college laboratory with the reputable scientist to get back to his work and to leave Dr. Sycamore to his.

He then rested for the evening and went back into the jungle at the crack of dawn to attempt to capture the winged monkey for the Zoological Museum in the States with the collapsible cage apparatus he kept in his backpack, or at the very least obtain photos of the creature for the world to see not only a rare species, but a new modern mammal mutation. He in addition wanted to see if one of the Scientists or Zoologists he knew in the United States would work with him to study the cause and origin of the mutation.

Ezel searched desperately day after day for the mysterious creature to no avail. After weeks of camping in the jungle, fighting off countless annoying and blood sucking insects, avoiding deadly run ins with wild animals, enduring inclement weather and uncomfortable conditions, Ezel was on the verge of giving up on the possibility of ever seeing the creature again and even begin thinking maybe he did imagine it like the Africans he saw gathered when he made his way out of the jungle stated he did, due to his fatigue and over excitement of a possible new find.

Just as he started to give up the search, head back to civilization and signal for his pilot to pick him up in the small aircraft to travel back to the States with disappointment of no new find to bring back, he begin hearing animal sounds like he had never heard in his extensive career as a Chief Zoological Explorer. It was a combination of monkey sounds and strange bird calls simultaneously (ooh ooh ooh eee eee eee aah aah aah, mixed with loud chirps and many other animal sounds he never heard before.)

As he followed stiffly with his eyes and ears the direction of the sounds, he begin to see with amazement a host of the other mutants all throughout the thick leafed jungle. No longer frozen in fear of the cross breeds, he was now in awe and astonishment of them, but yet still baffled by the mystifying change in nature. Ezel lifted his camera from his neck, zoomed in and begin snapping pictures profusely of the twisted creatures.

He was not equipped - nor did he come with the manpower to physically capture all the animals and was unsure of his safety with approaching them; therefore, Ezel took the photos he snapped back to Dr. Sycamore who gave a long pause after viewing the images and calmly stated that no one would believe the pictures are authentic and would just accuse him of photo shopping the images. The mastermind scientist then cautioned Ezel to not go back into the jungle or he may not make it back out alive and to, "leave the creatures be". He also sneeringly told Ezel, "I informed you of the possibility of this", and went on with his other lab work.

The Chief Explorer just blamed the lack of excitement and nonchalant response on the long time Scientist as aging and losing the love and curiosity he once had for science and research during his prime. Ezel took the photos back to Michigan and showed them to the Curator at the Zoological Museum who refused to print and hang what he considered bogus photos. The Curator accused Ezel of doctoring the images due to him being unable to secure another rare find, and stated he refuses to hang phony photos down the halls of the highly regarded museum walls.

Ezel was devastated that he was thought of as being dishonest after such a long reputable career with the museum. Ezel looked the Curator directly in the eyes and asked, "Have you ever known my work to have a lack of credibility for the 22 years I've been in this field or the time I've been with this museum?" The Curator turned away as he mumbled, "Desperate times sometimes cause for desperate measures".

Ezel walked away hurt and disappointed, but did not give up. He went to other museums to see if they would test the legitimacy of the photos and give him an opportunity to display his work. He even offered them to send someone with him; however, they were not willing to spend their resources or risk their reputation on what they thought of as fraud. He was turned down by all of the others as well. Ezel saw no other way but to go back to Africa with his own assistants to try and capture a few of the animals. One of the assistants were skeptical, but curious, the other believed and trusted in Ezel because he knew of the Chief Explorer's long history of work and impeccable reputation. The men headed back to the African jungle armed with needles, tranquilizers, collapsible wheeled cages, huge bags and net guns. The 3 men team was prepared to fight their way through the thick brush in the middle of the jungle with machetes and to camp out for as long as it took in order to capture the offspring of the cross bred creatures.

Dr. Sycamore learned of Ezel's planned return the day before he was to be there and informed the armed Africans he hired to let him know if Ezel's aircraft is spotted trying to land. Dr. Sycamore paid the gunmen to cease any attempts of Ezel to go into their jungle and went on and on about how "Those arrogant Americans always think they can go anywhere they want and have anything they please".

After Ezel and his assistants touched down and begin treading through the jungle, they noticed they were being followed and camouflaged themselves night after night until the African gunmen turned around refusing to go further into the thick, mysterious, dangerous jungle - especially after hearing rumors of the modern mutants and of people who went deep in and never came back out. The African gunmen falsely reported back to Dr. Sycamore that they did not see Ezel and his crew going into the jungle.

Ezel led the men back to the location where the mutants were after they noticed they were no longer being trailed. He discretely stuck tiny brown and green tacks at the base of certain trees to help him remember his way through to the remote location and used colors that would blend in with the forest so no one else could follow his path. They had finally arrived to the animals' enclave. He and his crew saw "gelephants" (giraffes with elephant bodies), "snats" (snake heads and torsos with rat tail ends), "winged monkeys", "frizards" (frogs with lizard heads), "zions" (lions with zebra stripes) and "aarzelles", (aardvarks with heads of gazelles). The men tranquilized the adult mammals and captured the infants of each creature to take back to the States.

They made it out of the jungle undetected and back on the aircraft they had waiting tucked away and camouflaged. After throwing the huge jungle leaves off the plane they used to conceal it, they headed back to the U.S. with the offspring of the cross bred creatures. On their way back, they surmised many hypothetical theories of how the animals came into existence and stared unbelievably at every single detail of each one.

Ezel then headed back to the zoological museum he works for with the small mutants, some of which did not survive the trip, but were still preserved. The Curator was in disbelief and offered Ezel an apology as well as top dollar for the animals, an amount he has not received in his entire career at the museum or as a Chief Zoologist at any museum for that matter.

Word eventually got out and the Zoological Museum's popularity increased 1,000 fold! Other museums wanted in on the frenzy; people from all over the world traveled in to get a glimpse of the unbelievable freaks of nature. All of the previous places and people who doubted Ezel were now blowing his phone up; he could barely empty his voice messages before they were full again.

Scientist, Biologists, Zoologists, Paleontologist, Anthropologists and all other types of ologists flew in from all over the globe to collaborate and try to make sense of the mythical like creatures. The top scientists from each of the aforementioned fields traveled to Africa to get to the bottom of the mystery mutants.

After months and months of examining the animals in their African habitat, no one has yet to observe any cross mating taking place and begin getting suspicious about the origins of the animals. African scientists at the only local scientific college lab in the area are being secretly investigated by the other scientists and still nothing has been uncovered or discovered. Some of the American scientists then come up with an idea and try a new avenue. They have a few top science students from prestigious universities apply for the African college as international students with the underlying intent of finding out any information on Dr. Sycamore and his college laboratory that he practically lives in, under the guise of wanting to broaden their scientific studies in the natural African habitat under his tutelage.

Several months have passed and the mutants in the Zoological Museum in the States have caused more breaking news; they have grown exponentially. The hormonal imbalance of the mutants are taking effect, they are becoming abnormally large and appear to have signs of rabies. The mutants have gone mad and have broken through the thick glass enclosures amongst hundreds of visitors attacking everyone and everything in their path! They escape through the doors and windows of the museum and eventually have to be put down in the middle of the streets surrounding the museum after millions of dollars in property damage, lives being lost and people being injured during the wild never seen before stampede. Police, coroners, ambulances and wildlife commissioners are all available to take control of the situation. News crews and helicopters were also on the scene filming and reporting the calamity.

Meanwhile, back in Africa at the college lab, there has been a lead. One of the U.S. students noticed Dr. Sycamore leaving a secret door with a digital coded lock as the student went to obtain an extra beaker after his fell to the floor and shattered as he was working late in the lab. After Dr. Sycamore left for the evening, not knowing the student was there hiding after hours, he stealthily awaited under one of the stations until he hears the Professor pull out of the small rocky parking lot and goes immediately to the secret door that is staged as a gigantic wall-picture filled with colorful glow in the dark science illustrations of beakers, test tubes, DNA strands, flasks, funnels, microscopes and chemical splash goggles.

He quietly calls and informs the other 2 students that night that he was still inside and would install the hidden cameras they were waiting for the opportunity to install to capture whatever they could find to get to the bottom of what was going on. He used the micro sized cameras to sit at an angle where he could see Dr. Sycamore enter the alarm codes to the entrance door of the lab and the secret picture door.

The students came into the college lab the following morning and played it cool for several days until they were able to capture the entry code to the "secret door", which Dr. Sycamore never entered while they were present in order to keep its existence confidential. Zach had to spend the night inside to not set off the alarm by leaving, but Dr. Sycamore did not notice he never went home. He thought they all left since they all said their goodbyes. After capturing and reviewing the footage, they learn the codes and return to the lab in the middle of the night to secretly enter.

As the students quietly enter the disguised door, they are amazed at what they have discovered! There are anesthetized monkeys, zebras, snakes, rats and aardvarks. They look around the locked room and find a manuscript on how to strategically withdraw DNA and insert it into another animal to cross breed and create the mystery mutants. The students also find baby mutants being artificially nursed by machinery until they are large enough to be let into the jungle.

They open another door inside the secret room that they almost missed since it looked like part of the wall, until one of the students heard an eerie noise coming from that direction. As they slowly crack open the heavy door, they find a small dark area full of haggardly looking African teen girls staring quietly and fearfully back at them. Half of them were impregnated and the others were due to be inseminated with the various male animal sperm and endure a period of gestation and deliver the final project that Dr. Sycamore has been working on for years to figure out how to create after practicing with the existing animal mutants. He broke the genetic code! He had named on the top of his manuscript, which was indeed his ultimate project, "The Book of Genetic Engineering".

The American students freed the African girls who spoke a dialect they did not understand and called authorities who came to the rescue and gave the teen girls immediate medical attention. Each adolescent female was permanently branded with a letter on her belly, which was discovered during their medical examinations. The teens each had one of the following letters on their abdomens: A, S, AA, L, M, R, E, or G; each letter beginning with the letter of every sample confiscated from the lab that turned out to be matching DNA of the seminal fluid from each animal, (alligator, snake, aardvark, lion, monkey, rat, elephant and gazelle). Dr. Sycamore had a rough draft documenting the entire procedure from beginning to end of the process to transfer the semen to the teens' eggs from the animals for in vitro fertilization and the secret component he used to ensure its success.

Additionally, the final chapter of the document detailed the beginning stages of how to attempt to mutate and merge an infant human with each jungle animal, as well as a list of the names and addresses of expecting African females and their due dates, which it was discovered he was preparing to genetically engineer the newborns once they were delivered. The highly regarded reputable science professor was then confronted, arrested at his home during the middle of the night and has been now deemed by the towns people as the "Mad Scientist", and the science community labeled him the "The Bio-hacker".

The anesthetized animals were eventually liberated and led back into their habitats. The college lab was completely destroyed by the natives who were furious and disgusted with the plans to kidnap, begin mutating expecting infants, as well as with the kidnapped teens who were being held hostage to impregnate and who were already pregnant after being inseminated with animal semen. The semi animal fetuses some of the teenage girls were impregnated with were all aborted. Prior to terminating the pregnancies, evidence was gathered in the form of ultrasounds, which showed 3D images of a combination of human and animal body parts developing. The aborted part human and part animal fetuses were also jarred and preserved in formaldehyde for research; however, the scientists and doctor did not reveal to anyone that was done.

After Dr. Sycamore was detained and the images were leaked and released, the towns' people went haywire. He was assassinated and never made it to court to stand trial. His parents finally broke their silence and spoke out after being threatened and having to move from the village.

They gave an account on how as a child, their son grew up as the intellectual odd ball of the family who excelled in his studies, especially in the sciences and how he took a special liking to his animal toys as a young boy. How he would play with his plastic and rubber toy animals by switching the body parts and lining them up perfectly on his dresser, which also had various paraphernalia that he created from miscellaneous objects around the house to look like a makeshift science laboratory workstation.

His mother detailed how she would snap the animals' body parts back to the animal they actually belonged to after he had unsnapped them and put them on the incorrect animals, initially thinking maybe her son was just having fun for the moment and forgot to put them back, but she would find them all put back exactly how he had them prior to her fixing them as soon as he noticed the change. Although it annoyed her, she just let him have fun with them how he wanted since she figured he was doing no harm by altering their body parts.

Dr. Sycamore's mother and father detailed how he had his rubber toy snake bodies crossed with rat tail ends that he used a safety pin to attach, monkeys with bird wings configured, elephant bodies with giraffe necks, frogs with lizard heads, lions with zebra stripes and aardvarks with the heads of gazelles.

His mother described how as a youth, the doctor would use her nail polish to paint the lions with zebra stripes and use glue or tape for parts that did not stay snapped or pinned on. Mrs. Sycamore also describes how after cleaning under her son's bed one morning when he was at school, she found 2 of his sister's toy dolls' heads; one was attached to an alligator body and one to his toy cheetah torso. A third doll was found in his closet and the torso was attached to a giraffe's head and neck. He had a fascination with altering nature. Dr. Sycamore was a maniacal monster in the making and no one ever noticed or gave it a second thought, until it was too late.

(Wisdom is wonderful, but can be used in wicked ways.)

KILLER BEES

(CHAPTER 6)

Ryan was in high school doing very well, and his social life was also flourishing with many friends and associates who loved to be around him due to his funny nature and loving spirit. He had an after school job so he was able to save for an older model vehicle that he wanted. He worked for half of the school year before he had enough money to purchase it. It did not run well, but he liked the body style and has a family member who works on vehicles as a shade tree mechanic that could help him with it.

The car sat in someone's backyard under a tree for years with a for sale sign placed in the windshield. He spotted it one day when he was visiting with a friend after school. He and the friend knocked on the owner's door to inquire; an elderly lady answered stating it was her late husband's and it has been back there for the last 3-4 years just "collecting dust and rust".

She allowed the boys to take a look at it. The thick layer of dust all over it appeared to be about a half an inch thick, one of the windows were stuck half-way down, a huge thick spider web was attached to the side mirror, and when they started the engine it took several attempts, but it eventually cranked. It made a sound that was evident that it needed a lot of work; however, this was enough for Ryan to know he would like to have it. The elderly lady quoted him a very reasonable price since she really just wanted it out of her yard.

He asked could she hold it for him, she said she would, but he would have to put a small amount down for her to do so to prove that he is serious just in case someone else came by wanting it. Ryan went to the ATM and brought her back $100 to hold it until he saved enough to purchase it.

Half of the school year had passed, Ryan finally had the amount the elderly lady wanted for the old school car. He was elated; he called her and told her he would be over this weekend to pick it up. As he rolled it out of the driveway in neutral until it cranked and slowly drove toward his destination to make sure it didn't cut off, he was ecstatic the whole way there. He could not wait to wash the exterior and drive it to school Monday morning. He planned on deep cleaning the interior the following weekend after his uncle helped him tune it up and tighten up a few more things in the engine to make it run smoother.

Monday morning arrived. Ryan begins his day on his way to school in his "new" vehicle with his best cologne on and the music blasting playing his favorite tunes during the ride. His uncle had advised him to not drive it yet, but told him if he was going to do so anyway, to at least drive it slowly in order to not be too rough on it until they could get a tune up and see what else it needed the following weekend. Of course, being an adolescent, he chose the latter.

As Ryan was riding down Main Street headed to school, he started to hear buzzing in one of his ears, so he fanned the annoying critter away. He then started to hear buzzing in the opposite ear, then fanned it away again. He then started to hear buzzing in both ears and saw a bee hovering around his face. He begin to pick up speed in the car as he noticed several bees were attempting to sting him as he was driving down the busy street in hopes they would be blown out the window from the excessive wind and so he could get to school faster to exit the vehicle.

He glanced in the rearview mirror and noticed the car was full of what looked like hundreds of bees that all started to swarm him. He was screaming and fanning and speeding up the street trying to get the bees off of him! The car begins to smoke and he started to swerve while trying to fight off the bees. Other motorists were honking and yelling at him as he was speeding and swerving.

The bees begin stinging him all over his body - head to legs while he continued in pursuit to his destination at school to get help there while manually rolling down the windows more and more hoping the bees that didn't get blown out of the window would fly out on their own. Other drivers were getting out of the way and jumping on their phones calling the police to inform them of what they saw as a reckless or drunk driver.

Ryan finally arrived on school grounds, by now he has lumps and red marks covering his entire body from bee stings. He runs the car into the front door of the school and hopped out yelling for help, smacking and sweeping himself all over trying to stop the vicious bee attack. He eventually fell to the ground flailing and wailing, "Get them off of me!" Fellow students see what is going on, some of them back away in silent horror, others ran the opposite direction screaming and some run to his defense.

Several of the guys begin stumping the hundreds of bees off of his body trying to kill them while they are still stinging and attacking him, as well as now attacking several other students who were nearby. This goes on for several minutes before teachers hear the commotion and rush out to assist. The teachers were screaming at the top of their lungs at the students who were trying to help telling them to "Stop kicking him!"

He began to stop fighting and lied there lifeless as the paramedics and EMTs who also answered the call arrived. The adults started to pull other students off of him and yell to them that they are harming him more by stomping the bees off of him. They rushed Ryan to the hospital and while en route they discover he had severe trauma from the stomping as well as from the bee attack. The few other students, who were also stung by a few of the bees, were treated by the school nurse and turned out to be fine.

The EMTs looked into the vehicle after the paramedics whisked Ryan away and found 2 huge hives in the back corner of the roof of the car with only a few bees left. They were defending what they believed was there territory and their queen bee to the detriment of Ryan. Some of his schoolmates tried to help, but made matters worse when the only solution they saw during the traumatic and horrific chaotic event was kicking the bees off of him to stop the severe stinging attack.

Everyone learned the extent of Ryan's injuries. 2 of his teeth were knocked out, he had a black eye, 1 of his ribs were broken, he suffered a concussion and had to obtain sutures in his head all from his peers who were trying to help. He also sustained swelling throughout his body from the bee stings in conjunction with the kicking, and discoloration all over his body from bruises. He had a fever, vomiting, and severe weakness as a result of the bee venom. He had countless bee stingers lodged in his skin throughout his body that doctors removed with sterile tweezers. Ryan complained while in the hospital bed that his body was itching so bad he just wanted to have alcohol poured all over him to stop the itching no matter how much it may burn.

The doctors gave him antihistamine and pain pills to make him more comfortable for his hospital stay. They also explained to him that the bee attack could have killed him. Many of the students and teachers came to visit bringing him balloons, cards and flowers. He eventually was released from the hospital and was told he would make a full recovery and be able to return to school in a few weeks.

The school staff used this as a learning opportunity an educated the entire school about how to handle a swarm of bees attacking by calling in a Bee Expert to inform the students of the do's and don'ts. The local news also discussed ways to thwart and handle bee attacks since the incident made headlines.

The Bee Expert discussed how bees will do anything to defend their hive and colony and how a beehive can be disturbed when there is loud noise, strong smells, or if it is being poked. He went on to explain how bees are attracted to movement and crushed bees emit a smell that will attract more bees, which is why Ryan was attacked so severely. He had the music up loud driving to school, the vehicle would bounce when he hit a bump in the road equivalent to a poke to the bees; he had on his loud cologne that day and he was flailing his arms and smacking his body trying to get the bees away from him crushing some of the bees in the process.

Ryan did everything he was not supposed to do in the presence of a mass bee attack. This may have been prevented or severely reduced if Ryan attempted to clean the interior of the car prior to driving and noticed them then, had he gotten out of the car immediately instead of continuing to drive - which he later stated he was in shock and was not thinking, or if he would have known the way to get away from a bee swarm, which is to run into the wind until you seek shelter since humans can usually outrun bees and the wind from running will make it harder for them to keep pace with you. He went on to explain how quickly seeking shelter will shut most of the bees out.

The Beekeeper further pointed out that even if it's makeshift shelter such as a vehicle, a blanket, bushes, etc.

it will help - and how to avoid getting into water to escape a bee attack, because if they are killer bees, they will wait until you come up for air then begin their attack again.

Words of Wisdom:

Sometimes valuable lessons are learned from the misfortune of others.

LOVER BOY

(CHAPTER 7)

"He is sooo cute!", Which is what all of the elementary aged school girls said to each other as they walked through the halls going to the cafeteria, physical education class or on a restroom break and they would see him. "He's fine as wine!", Is what all the high school girls would say about him as they spotted him in the breezeway passing classes.

Darnell knew he was one of the most striking guys in the whole school. He had known this since he had all of the elementary school girls crushing on him, and he took full advantage of it by the time he was high school age. He would play the high school girls like a piano. He claimed no less than 5 girls at a time as his girlfriends. They all knew he was no good, but most of them didn't care as long as they got a piece of the most attractive, athletic, best dressed, and coolest guy in school. Other guys gained cool points by just hanging out with him.

He was so charming and cool even the female and male teachers would let him get away with more than the other students. His first year of high school in the 9th grade, he was out of school for a whole week when he told his mother he was not feeling well. His mother informed the school that Darnell was ill and would return to school next week when he is feeling better. While he was out, many of the female students sent electronic cards via text message and social media, balloons and even his favorite candy via snail mail and home visits. His 5 girlfriends also came by to visit with him at various times crossing each other's paths coming and going giving each other the evil eye as they bypassed one another.

After that week passed by, Darnell was finally better and went back to school. Things were back to normal as usual and semester after semester passed with Darnell continuing with his player, bad boy ways. He also had a hot temper and his girlfriends and male friends knew not to remotely say or do anything to make him upset. He eventually graduated high school and went on to college. His bad boy, hot tempered, player ways still remained constant, although his friends calmed theirs down realizing it was time to grow up and stop leading the ladies on. However, this time around Darnell could only play 2 girls at a time since he realized college girls were more mature and less likely to put up with obviously being toyed with.

Darnell also begin skipping school, smoking marijuana, drinking and partying a lot, resulting in him eventually being kicked off of the basketball team and flunking out of college. He started chasing even more skirts, as well as making babies left and right with various women and very little means to pay a penny of child support. He would only talk to the caramel complected, physically fit and shapely girls with long curly or wavy hair. This became the physical criteria the girls had to meet to be a part of, "Dee's She's", as Darnell would call them.

As the years went pass, the amount of children Darnell was fathering begin to increase, as well as the women who were bearing them. They were willing to put up with all of Darnell's idiocy, at least temporarily, because he was handsome, dressed nice, was athletic, had madd swag, kept a shiny new car and always had spending money. Little did they know, it was because although he had reached 30 by now, he was still living at home with his mother who didn't require him to pay any bills.

He would also get by living house to house with different women until one of them eventually became fed up, put him out, and he would go back home to his mother's revolving door until the next "caramel cutie", (as Darnell would refer to them) would take him in, which was never very long with Darnell's good looks and prowess with women.

This continued to go on for years; he would sometimes even recycle his children's mothers along with meeting new women as well. Darnell would occasionally see some of his 9 kids when he was living with one of their mothers or when the holidays rolled around, which is when his mother would demand to see all of her grandchildren.

Darnell was beginning to fall apart with his partying, player ways and lifestyle of getting high. He started lacing his marijuana with cocaine and drinking heavier. It eventually caused him to have his car repossessed, he ceased dressing nice and used the extra money he had solely on drugs and alcohol. He finally secretly checked himself into a rehabilitation facility for help with his substance abuse issues and his anger management problems, which was also getting worse.

Once he was halfway through the treatment program, he finally confided in his mother, whom he was very close to, about his drugs and heavy alcohol use and as he knew she would, she maintained her undying support. Darnell admitted to his mother he was embarrassed to tell her initially because he knew how highly she thought of him. He begin speaking more personally with his Substance Abuse Counselor, Ms. Pruitt as she gained his trust over time in treatment. He admitted to her that he had never felt as comfortable telling his problems to anyone as he did with her and disclosed how he always buried his sad or negative feelings and thoughts in order to maintain his image.

Ms. Pruitt was Darnell's physical type, but he respected her and knew not to cross the line with her and surprisingly kept it professional - only complimenting her once. She was open-minded, non-judgmental, made him feel relaxed and let him know it was OK to share his true feelings and would never have to worry about anything he said ever being repeated.

Ms. Pruitt asked him what was he suppressing with his excessive drug and alcohol use and negative behavior.

Darnell, mister hardcore ladies' man, begin divulging with tears pouring out of his eyes and down his cheeks the event that led him down his path of destruction. He said to the Counselor in a serious, solemn, tone, "I have never revealed this information to anyone, but I have grown to trust and admire you".

Darnell took a deep breath and let it all out while Ms. Pruitt gave her undivided attention. "I was raped as a 14 year old boy by 3 white men as I was walking home alone from school one day through a short cut I always used near an area that was full of bushes and trees. They jumped out of a pickup truck with huge tires and a loud muffler, I ran as fast as my feet would carry me, but was caught and rushed to the ground. 2 of them at a time held me down while one would penetrate me until they were all done. I initially tried to fight, scream and yell, but I was being subdued by 3 fully grown men and my strength could not compare. I could never come to grips or understand why this happened to me. I continued to have so many women and only date the ones most people see as the most desirable because it is my way of coping and compensating for what I endured as a 14 year old boy."

"Continuing to have so many women and children, sadly over the years in some sick twisted way has helped me with what they took away from me, my manhood. This is the only way I know how to deal with this trauma I live with every day. However, now that I'm evolving mentally, emotionally and spiritually, I now know that way of coping is warped. I also begin getting high as a way to suppress the thoughts of those 3 white men taking me. It seems the older I get, the more vivid the thoughts become and the more frequent they enter my consciousness."

"I have destroyed my children's lives by bringing them into this world and not being there for them. I have also devastated their mother's lives by playing with their hearts and minds as a way to deal with my own personal issues; and I have damaged myself by poisoning my body with drugs and alcohol as a way to suppress the thoughts of that dreadful day after school that I will never forget."

Darnell went on to reveal to Ms. Pruitt how he took a week off when he was in high school and told his mother and friends he was ill from a stomach ache - feigning diarrhea and vomiting so that his mother would believe him following the gang rape. "I was too sore physically and screwed up mentally to get out of bed for a week, but didn't know how to tell anyone the truth about what happened until today, almost 25 years later. This incident is also the reason why my anger management issues increased and I recently came to this epiphany while seeing you for therapy".

Time goes on and Darnell continues therapy and successfully completes Substance Abuse Treatment and Anger Management classes. He is still a work in progress learning to deal with his past and move forward without being angry, using women or drugs and alcohol to cope. He still keeps in touch with Ms. Pruitt and tells her he is not sure if he can or will ever inform another soul about that incident, but feels liberated now that he is no longer carrying that lifelong secret around that was beginning to burden him more and more as time passed.

❖ **A thought to ponder**: One never knows the reasoning of someone's behavior; they don't get a pass for hurting others, but there is usually always a motive.

P.M.S
PHYSICAL TO MENTAL SICKNESS
(CHAPTER 8)

It all started out normal, the typical American family living in the outskirts of the city with 2 ½ kids, a fenced in home, toys in the backyard - nothing outside the ordinary. Liza, the mother was a homemaker who took pride in rearing her twin boys and was excited about the child on the way. The father, Liza's husband was a well-established businessman who provided well for his family. There were a lot of late nights at the office, but his wife never complained since she knew working late was how they kept their comfortable lifestyle of a nice home, decent vehicles, fun weekends and annual vacations abroad.

Years pass of the day to day routine of rearing children and her husband furthering his career. This required business trips, which kept him away from home for 3-4 days at a time a couple of times per month. Liza eventually begin growing increasingly tired of her husband not being home enough to spend quality time with her and the children, but continued not complaining since he made sure she and the children were well taken care of. She didn't mind the late work nights, but the multiple days away so often are what got to her.

Liza being pregnant with her 3rd child has approached the end of her third trimester and is ready for delivery. Derrick, her husband, was there for the birth of their daughter whom they named Lyric, after Liza, since she used to enjoy writing music; they rejoiced about having a seemingly healthy baby and took her home to her beautifully decorated, colorful, artful room.

Her husband took 2 weeks off of work to bond and help out with the new baby before returning to his job. Everything went back to normal with Liza taking care of the children while her husband Derrick went back to working late nights at the office and 3-4 day business trips 2-3 times per month. Lyric eventually was due for her first wellness checkup. The baby came home cranky and uncomfortable due to having shots and blood work, but seemed otherwise fine.

Several days go past and Liza receives a phone call from the pediatrician informing her that she needed to come in to speak with her. She asked Dr. Garner why she could not speak to her over the phone. The doctor stated it is best to explain everything face to face. Liza asked the doctor what was wrong. Dr. Garner expressed how it's best practice to inform patients about any information face to face. She informed her doctor she would be in first thing in the morning. Dr Garner told Liza to make sure she brings Lyric. She stayed up all night worrying about what the doctor could possibly want to speak to her about. Her husband tried to assure her that everything would be fine and she should get some sleep. The morning finally approaches, Derrick went to work, Liza dropped the twins off at their kindergarten class while she and the baby went to see the pediatrician.

Dr Garner had a look on her face that told Liza something was not right. The doctor informed her that Lyric's blood tests came back and she tested positive for HIV. Liza was completely confused, irate, hurt, and every other mixed emotion screaming how did this happen?! How is this possible?! Why was this not detected during my pregnancy?! The doctor calmly told Liza that her last checkup was when she was 7 1/2 months pregnant and everything was fine from the specimens at that time, and if she was recently infected it can take up to 3 months before any HIV test can detect the presence of the virus from antibodies in the blood.

The doctor informed Liza that she needs to tell her husband to get tested and asked her if she has been with anyone else outside of her marriage. She scornfully told Dr. Garner that she has NEVER cheated on her husband, then snatched her baby's diaper bag off of the counter and made a sharp turn with the baby stroller as she forcefully walked out of her office.

Liza drove home seething with fear, rage, and disgust about her and the baby's new horrifying health statuses. She paced the floor of her home most of the day waiting for her husband to get home to confront him since she was unable to reach him at the office due to him being in meetings all day.

When Derrick finally came home, Liza walked up to him 1 inch away from his face and asked him, "What the hell have you been up to behind my back?" Derrick acted confused, begins sweating and asked her, "What are you talking about? What is wrong with you?" Liza then showed Derrick the documentation for both she and Lyric that read, "The blood specimen you submitted was reactive for HIV antibodies".

Tears begin pouring down Derrick's eyes; he dropped to his knees hugging Liza around her thighs wailing and begging for her forgiveness. He then begins divulging his double life and admitting how he has wanted to tell her so many times, but never got up the courage to do so that he has been sexually involved with a man. Liza pushed Derrick off of her legs, begin throwing things around the house at him while yelling and crying for him to get out. Derrick dodged the vase, lamp, and a picture frame as he made it out of the front door.

Liza went to check on the children who were crying in the bedroom after hearing the commotion. She calmed them down and told them everything was fine. After she put them to bed, she stayed up all night sobbing and unable to sleep due to millions of thoughts running through her mind about her and the newborn's health, her twin boys, her marriage, and flags she ignored throughout the marriage. The next morning after dropping the twins off at school, she called around to multiple law offices and made an appointment to speak with a Divorce Attorney.

As time goes on, Liza gets adjusted to being a single mother and finds part time employment to supplement the child support for her 3 children. She focuses all of her attention on being a great mother while continuing to ensure she and Lyric take their daily medications for their diagnosis. The twin boys eventually graduate high school after Lyric enters middle school. Liza sits Lyric down and finally explains to her since she feels she is at an age where she can understand now, how she has been taking medication for an illness called Human Immunodeficiency Virus, better known as HIV and not vitamins as she has been told all of these years. Liza explained to her daughter how her father passed the illness to them and how they will have to live with it for the rest of their lives, but can still live a normal lifestyle as long as they continue to take their antiretroviral medication and stay healthy.

Lyric eventually starts high school, is more mature and curious, and begins to research her HIV diagnosis. She learns that she can pass the virus to anyone she becomes intimate with without protection, how it can also be passed through blood and breast milk, and how the virus cannot survive in urine, saliva, tears, or sweat since they do not have enough white blood cells for the virus to grow.

Lyric continues successfully in high school with perfect attendance and honor roll while continuously growing angry and hiding that emotion about her lifelong disease. She becomes a senior in high school and has received several letters from different universities for scholarships due to her academic excellence since elementary school and scoring in the highest percentile on every test the school has required her to take. However, Lyric still lives with bitterness, unhappiness and feeling that life has been unfair to her as she secretly lives with her diagnosis.

Lyric develops a promiscuous personality and becomes intimate with several boys at the school during her senior year. They were the ones who were well known for having the most "friends with benefits" with the girls in the school. Neither of the boys used protection nor did she disclose her status to them. She goes on to pursue her education further by attending one of the universities that gave her a scholarship. She continues to do well academically while still battling her health misfortune emotionally and increasingly is having a harder time coping with her unfortunate circumstance.

She continues her promiscuity with the college guys - graduates and goes on to have a successful career. However, Lyric does not slow down or cease with her sexual behavior, it actually increases and she sleeps with countless men during her adulthood as well, all unprotected and knowing that she is putting everyone at risk starting from the high school boys, to the college guys, and now the adult men. Lyric is unconcerned with the results of her actions and continues this behavior.

One of the men she has been having an intimate fling with, Walt, happened to be speaking with an older buddy of his about his encounter with Lyric. He informed this close friend how he had been having a flaming fling with a younger chick named Lyric who was the best he has ever had. He went on describing when and where they were having their rendezvous and how kinky it would get. His friend was relishing in the conversation and amazed with some of the accounts of the when, where, and how of the sexual encounters.

His buddy was deeply engaged enjoying every single detail; however, it was as if something struck him out of nowhere. He paused for a moment…he asked Lyric's age and profession. Walt informed him she was a 25 year old Accountant. His friend stared at Walt for what seemed like an eternity with a grim look on his face; Walt asked him, "Why are you looking at me like that man?" His friend said to him in a slow solemn monotone voice. "Walt, I have only known of one Lyric in my 50 years of life. She should be about mid-twenties now, is in the Accounting field, went to school on a scholarship due to her high academic achievement and was a patient of my wife's until she turned 18".

His friend asked if her last name was Livingston, Walt said it was. His friend told him of a story from 25 years ago that his wife confided in him about of a Lyric Livingston who was born infected with HIV due to her father having sexual relations with a man, catching it, then passing it on to his wife and their unborn child, which happened to be Lyric. Walt slowly stood up and walked out of the front door without saying a word.

Walt slid into his car and immediately called his doctor's office for an appointment for testing. The doctor told him he could come in first thing Monday morning of next week. The tests eventually came back and Walt tested positive for HIV. He called law enforcement to report Lyric. She was arrested, her face was all over the news and multiple men dating back to her high school years came forward divulging that they had also been sexually involved with her without protection or without being informed of her HIV status. Lyric was charged with 9 counts of Criminal Transmission of HIV. Although there were about 19 men she had been with, the others may not have come forward due to shame or not wanting their wives and girlfriends to know they were cheating. She plead guilty and received a 10 year sentence for each count causing her to spend the rest of her natural life in prison.

Lyric confessed after sentencing that she felt since she was dealt an unfair hand, others should be too, especially the men who just want to have sexual encounters and not want commitment and were cheating on their significant others to have flings with her. With no remorse, Lyric stated before being hauled off in her shackles and orange Department of Corrections apparel behind the courtroom doors, "They all got what they deserved!" Her heart had become cold and hardened over the years being that she could not get past being an innocent victim of her father's transgressions.

Words of Wisdom: Never allow something you cannot change take control of your life, it can lead to bitterness, poor decisions, and major consequences.

Scared Silent

(CHAPTER 9)

They lived a normal life, to outsiders that is. They had 4 children, were a married, hardworking, uneducated low income couple. Sure they had their highs and lows like any other married couple. Their children were all born healthy and went to school daily just as they went to work daily. Tori, the mother, worked pressing clothes at a dry cleaning establishment, which paid slightly higher than Rick's job as a dish washer for one of the local food chain restaurants. The 2 younger children were in daycare, they were only 1 and 2 years of age. The 2 eldest children were ages 6 and 8. With a large family and not much income, the couple was always stressing over something, but lately the stress levels had been rapidly increasing.

Rick begin yelling at Tori for any minute reason, such as not giving him enough meat and potatoes on his plate or because she was allowing the kids to make too much noise while he was watching television. However, Tori would stand her ground and shout back about how she could use more help around the house, until one day she raised her voice to him and Rick smacked her so hard it sounded as if someone lit a firecracker. She could not believe her husband could do such a thing since he never put his hands on her before and only went as far as pointing his finger closely in her face during heated arguments.

She withdrew from him, but he apologized after a couple of weeks of the silent treatment and told her his stress was building up due to him working hard long hours every day, but still feeling like he cannot get ahead. Tori forgave her husband, he once again begin receiving her affection and things went back to their normal lifestyle of high stress, living check-to-check, 4 children to care for and getting by to the best of their ability.

After several months, the stress continued to increase and Rick escalated from shouting, pointing in Tori's face about small issues and the one time open-handed smack, to full-fledged physical beatings. Deep inside, he was harboring inadequacies, jealousy, and insecurities about being the man of the house and not being able to properly provide and contribute to the household. He paid half of the already low rent, and Tori paid the other half, as well as all of the utilities and purchased most of the groceries since Rick was unable to due to his hours being cut on his already low paying minimum wage job. Rick graduated high school, but had no additional education or training and Tori dropped out of school in the 10th grade to care for her first born child and work. They were high school sweethearts and did everything together.

Nevertheless, she was fed up with the abuse and packed up her and the children's belongings to escape to a woman's shelter after the beatings became longer and harder, causing her to hide constant black eyes with make-up and explain away bruises with lame excuses to her few friends, family, and co-workers.

After several weeks passed and Rick constantly leaving her voice messages and texts, Tori left the women's shelter wanting to give it one more chance with holding her family together and fearing she will not be able to make it completely alone financially. Rick was happy to have her and the children back home and showed his remorse by helping more with the kids and around the house. He also refrained from putting his hands on her.

However, that did not last very long. The frustration and depression of not being able to obtain a better paying job continued to weigh on Rick's conscious and the bitterness of seeing his neighbors and friends buy nice things sometimes with their extra money, others at his place of employment in different positions being able to go out to eat for lunch while he was only able to bring a pack of $.50 noodles or peanut butter and jelly sandwiches and his wife bringing in the most money even with her low paying wage was causing him to seethe with jealousy, envy, and anger.

It only took the small comment of Tori insisting that Rick cook dinner for the family this time around since she always does it and since he had a little more time being that she often worked over time and he only worked a 30 hour week to set him completely off and triggered him to begin beating her again. The kids would crouch in terror near the closest corners, in the closets or behind doors during the beatings. Rick even escalated to breaking glasses and pictures in the house as an extension of his rage.

Tori's family rarely came to her home since they grew to despise Rick, whose personality deteriorated over the years, and she hardly ever went to their homes except for holidays since she was busy with the kids and her husband seemed to have a problem with it when she went to visit them "too often". Rick was never very close with his family and had not visited or spoken with them in years. The kids' grades begin dropping in school and they grew more frightened of their father. They no longer jumped on his back when he came home from work or asked him to play with them, and Tori felt as if she was walking on broken glass whenever she came home not knowing when the next blow to the body, smack to the face or piece of furniture would come flying her way. She lived in absolute terror.

Despite her situation, Tori refused to call the police on Rick; especially after he threatened he would kill her once he was released from the county jail if she ever did. Tori continued to take the beatings for another 2-3 years before she came to the realization that she would be dead anyway if she continued to do nothing and stay with him. The poundings were not getting any easier to take, Tori begin receiving 2 black eyes instead of one, bruises turned into broken skin, and the children were collateral damage physically, mentally, and emotionally from the abuse.

She finally built up the courage to call 911 after Rick threw a vase at her during one of their heated arguments, and it ricocheted off the sofa when it missed her, bounced up and burst across one of the children's heads - shattering to the floor upon impact; fortunately and amazingly causing only a few scratches on the child and a few sparkles on the forehead when the child turned towards the light until the few pieces of glass were scraped off. When the police arrived, Rick was hauled off to jail and gave Tori this long intimidating stare straight into her eyes without mumbling a word and barely blinking from the time the cuffs were being put on until the time he walked down the front porch steps and pulled off in the back of the police car. Tori shivered with fear the whole time Rick was gone feeling only a few moments of peace here and there knowing he could not get to her... at least for now.

Rick was out on bail after a few weeks when his estranged family collaborated and came up with the bail money for him. He came home to find out the house was empty. Tori, fearing Rick's promise to end her life if she ever called law enforcement, had packed up as much as she could and moved across town. She felt she could not go much further since she had little money, knew no one outside of the city, was a high school dropout, and did not want to risk losing the only job she has ever had at the dry cleaners. Tori felt slightly safe since she told no one where she had moved to and informed the 2 older kids who always obeyed to do the same.

However, it was not long before Rick tracked Tori and the children down after calling every single elementary school in the entire city until he was able to locate the one his children were enrolled in. Tori did not inform the school staff of what was going on because she did not want them in her business or calling the Department of Children and Family Services on her, which she knew they would likely do. Once he knew he had the right school, Rick made his way up there right before the kids were due to be released for the day, sought his 2 elementary aged children out and secretly followed them home.

Once nightfall hit, he knocked on the door trying to apologize and talk to Tori promising that he had changed.

When she refused to open the door, he forced himself through the weakly secured front entrance and begin beating her harder than he had ever beat her before, stating a partial sentence with each blow. (PUNCH)- I told you, (PUNCH)- not to ever call the cops on me, (SMACK), and if you did (SMACK), I would kill you (KICK). The kids were all crying and frozen with fear while watching in terror as their mother was being beaten to a bloody pulp by their very own father.

Rick then pulled out a knife from his pocket and began stabbing Tori repeatedly while the kids screamed in fear helplessly. When the oldest child instinctively ran over to grab his arm screaming, "Daddy stop!" He just flung the child back across the room where the others were. Rick continued stabbing Tori until her helpless body stopped moving. He then nonchalantly walked out of the door, leaving her there to die on the living room floor. A neighbor came over after hearing unceasing screeching cries from the children and found all 4 of them curled about their mother's bloody body shouting her name

simultaneously, "mooommmmmyyyy!!!!!,
moooommmmmmmmmmmyyyyyyy!!!!!!".

The next door neighbor called 911, Tori was hauled off on a stretcher and after hours of trying to revive her, she incredibly survived the brutal assault and spent months recovering in the hospital's ICU. Social Workers had placed the kids into foster care until family members came forward volunteering to care for them while waiting for Tori to be released from the hospital. Following her discharge from the medical center, a few months later Tori was able to return to work and eventually reunited with her children.

As time passed, she noticed the eldest sister and brother had not spoken a word for days and was also told by her family that they had not spoken to anyone; not even each other, since they were in their care. However, the 2 youngest children were back to running and playing around like nothing happened. Tori figured that the silence was due to the trauma and believed they would be fine in a few more weeks once they see they are safe and no longer have to fear their father since his bail was too high to afford and he was facing over 25 years in prison for Attempted Murder, Assault, Breaking and Entering, and Child Endangerment.

The following school year Tori and the children's teachers noticed that Rick Jr. and Zaria, the two eldest of the 4, were still not uttering a single word. Social Services referred the children to a Psychologist. During the sessions, they did not speak with the Psychologist, only shaking their heads yes and no to certain questions and writing down answers if they were asked something. The Psychologist, Dr. Grince had observed enough from the children to come up with a diagnosis. She informed Tori that Rick Jr. and Zaria's conditions are referred to as Selective Mutism, and it is often caused by severe trauma, which is an extreme form of control for a child who can control so little else. However, Dr. Grince further explained how the children will usually speak again in situations which they feel comfortable; but it will be at their own pace and time frames, which can sometimes take months or years after witnessing such acute trauma as they have.

This information gave Tori hope for her children and so she went on with life as normal as she could in such a situation and the family adapted to the circumstances. Several years passed, Zaria and Rick Jr. eventually went on to high school and were placed in special classes since they still were not speaking.

After graduating high school, there was still no progress. Their social and daily living skills had ceased developing. Tori eventually put the 2 now young adults in an Assisted Living Facility geared to those who are unable to function normally in society completely on their own.

Zaria and Rick Jr. are currently in their mid-30's now, and still to this day, have never uttered another single word since the horrific incident they witnessed as children, which almost caused death to their mother. The 2 younger children progressed fine, but have since moved out of their home town, never to return and have not seen their siblings since they were placed in the Adult Facility.

➢ Although the events leading up to the incident is fictionalized, this attempted murder actually occurred, as well as the 2 children of the attempted murder victim remaining silent until this very day.

➢ Please leave when faced with any form of domestic violence, one never knows how it will escalate and people under estimate the lasting emotional and psychological damage it can cause.

<u>DOMESTIC VIOLENCE STATISTICS</u>

▪ On average, nearly 20 people per minute are physically abused by an intimate partner in the United States.

- 1 in 7 women and 1 in 25 men have been injured by an intimate partner

- 1 in 15 children are exposed to intimate partner violence each year.

- Children who witness domestic violence in their households are more likely to grow up and abuse or be abused.

- (NCADV – National Coalition Against Domestic Violence, ncadv.org - 2019)

"Sleep Disturbance"

(CHAPTER 10)

    She couldn't sleep a wink, so she sat in her favorite chair in the bedroom upstairs staring out the window during the middle of the night stargazing. She loved nature and was mesmerized by all it had to offer. No music, no TV, no phone, no internet - just basking in the silent night. She lived in a lower-middle-income neighborhood that was clean and quiet with very little crime. She had a bird's eye view into most of the neighbors' yards from her second floor bedroom window in her favorite chair, which happened to be a rocking chair, where she usually sat at night to read or stare at the stars before bedtime or on one of those rare nights when she had a difficult time sleeping.

She noticed all the comings and goings of the people on her block from this vantage point. She observed how one of the elderly neighbors left her window cracked all night so her cat could go in and out throughout the night as it pleased. She saw another neighbor's adolescent daughter sneaking out of the house after curfew a few times, but felt it wasn't her business to say anything. Other than that, there was rarely any activity in her neighborhood that time of night.

However, this particular night Karisma detected something strange. Directly across the street she paid attention to how her neighbor's thick round leafy bush continued to slightly sway back and forth, then side to side; at first she thought nothing of it being that Mrs. Little's cat always came in and out of that particular side of the window. Yet, she noticed the cat squeeze out the window and head in the opposite direction of the moving bush and wondered since it wasn't the cat, what was moving the large shrub. She ruled out the wind since the trees weren't blowing, but couldn't quite put her finger on it.

Karisma eventually ignored it and continued to enjoy the stars until she began to doze off rocking in her slightly creaking wooden rocking chair with her plush throw blanket wrapped around her shoulders and her soft fluffy pillow supporting her back. Her neighbor directly across the street, who was a bachelor and often came home late, pulled into his driveway and his bright red brake lights and squeaky suspension on his vehicle caused her to open her eyes. As he closed the car door and walked towards the side entrance of his home; a man dressed in all black jumped out of the large bush and caught him by surprise - grabbed him from the back by the neck and begin stabbing him profusely until he fell down limp in the driveway! His attempts to fight back were futile.

The man dressed in all black took a few steps backwards to walk away after briefly glaring at the victim's body, and then took off running up the street quickly and quietly. Karisma sat with her eyes wide open frozen in fear, then shock and panic set in. She eventually gathered her thoughts and called for help, however, it was too late, after the paramedics tried to revive him, they pronounced him dead on the scene. Karisma watched from her upstairs window for hours as they investigated the crime scene, ultimately zipping up the big black body bag he was finally stuffed in.

When questioned by detectives about what all she saw and if she recognized the perpetrator after one of them spotted her staring down from the upstairs window because of the glare of her nightlight and the streetlight, she reported that she had no idea who the guy was and although his figure was stocky, she told the detectives he appeared slim; although he was about the height of the victim, she informed the officers he was much taller.

It wasn't that she was fearful the culprit would come back to harm her, she was confident that would not happen. Her self-assurance came from knowing just who the offender was. And although he had this side to him that no one else knew existed, she was assured because this is the man who always protected her and would never harm her or allow detriment to come her way. Karisma felt it was her turn to return the favor despite the obligation to call the ambulance for help about her neighbor who lied helplessly in his driveway.

She was still in disbelief knowing the build and gate of the man walking away before fleeing was her very own brother, George. Rome, the now deceased neighbor, owed George money and was not attempting to pay him back; even when George told him he could pay in installments, he still didn't make any efforts, this caused George to feel angry, disrespected, and blown off.

However, George just sat back quietly for over a year and decided he would just cash out with Rome's life. George figured since Rome owing him money had been over a year ago, no one would ever seriously suspect him or tie it all together. He was right, when George was questioned by detectives after learning he frequented the neighborhood and was owed money by Rome at a point in time, George told them, "That was well over a year ago, I've gotten over that and moved on with my life" - they could not prove otherwise and so the case over time grew cold.

Life went on, George continued to go to work as if nothing happened and still visited with his sister often - as well as occasionally helping her out around the house. But she found herself unable to sleep at all since the incident. Karisma did not let George know she witnessed the murder and knew it was him. She tried to move past it, but it was causing her to lose weight, lose sleep, and have a high level of stress. She also began having nightmares. After 2 or 3 hours of sleep, she would wake up sweating with her hands in a defensive position screaming NOOOOO - at the top of her lungs most nights. Rome was haunting her in her sleep. He came to her almost every night dressed in all black and began to stab her until she woke up.

She dealt with the nightmares for almost a year before realizing she could not go on like this. The chronic sleep deprivation was causing cognitive problems, as well as physical health issues. She knew she had to do something. Over-the-counter sleeping pills helped her to doze off, but could not stop her from having or waking up from the nightmares every couple of hours.

Karisma already had suspicions of her brother harming another person years ago, before this incident. It happened 2 years after an altercation took place between the two. When a witness described the perpetrator, what he had on and how he wore his attire, it sounded so familiar; she was certain it was her brother when the eyewitness said the man had his socks pulled up over his pants legs.

Karisma had always noticed whenever George was going out to do yard work for her or odds and ends around the exterior of the house, he would always pull his socks up that way. When she asked him why one day, he said to prevent the bottom of his pants legs from getting caught up on something while he was working. It was this idiosyncrasy that led her to believe her suspicion was correct; that her brother was likely the perpetrator in an unsolved murder that happened not too far from his residence.

However, life continued and she never mentioned it to anyone or thought about it again. She knew this time it had to be different - if she didn't say anything, her night terrors would continue and George may go on to kill a third person over another minor dispute. As much as she loved her brother and did not want to see him imprisoned, she felt internally compelled to make an anonymous call to the police about the murder of her neighbor across the street, and so she did. A search warrant was issued for George's apartment and it revealed dried drops of blood on the side of his washing machine, which DNA tests later linked to Rome. George was eventually arrested, tried, and given life in prison. He never knew his sister turned him in, she wouldn't dare tell him - she knew it would break his heart knowing they only had each other all of these years and should have died with each other's secrets never being revealed.

The nightmares stopped after Karisma made the call; Rome's agitated spirit finally rested, which allowed her a little respite. However, she still felt internal turmoil for having turned her brother in and having to live with him serving a life sentence because of her anonymous phone call to authorities; she did not know how she would be able to endure living with herself, but knew had she not turned him in, the nightmares would have remained relentless since they had been going on for nearly a year with no signs of disappearing.

It was emotional torture living with her only sibling and the only person who had ever been there to protect her since she was a baby and since he was just 5-years-old while they were in and out of foster homes together, now living behind bars because of her phone call.

Eventually years had passed, it was now 6 ½ years into George's 28-year prison sentence and Karisma still was unable to rest well, although she was resting a little better over the years without the haunting nightmares of Rome viciously attacking her. However, she could not cease the thoughts of feeling that she was responsible for sentencing her brother to death by making that call since he would likely not live to see freedom again.

Karisma never went a day without thinking about her brother or crying herself to sleep every night about him being imprisoned and her being the one to turn him in. She was drowning in regret, was chronically stressed and had lost so much weight over the years that none of her clothes fit her properly anymore and she even looked physically ill. Her cheekbones protruded more than normal and the area around her eye sockets had become darkened and sunken in. The internal mayhem of simultaneous obligation and guilt never relented. Nevertheless, this particular night she got the best sleep she had in a very long time - there was no tossing, there was no turning and there was no waking up - ever. Karisma passed away in her sleep; she was only 45 years old. She died from a broken heart.

Broken Heart Syndrome- A temporary heart condition brought on by stressful situations which can mimic a heart attack. There's a disruption of the heart's normal pumping function that may be caused by the heart's reaction to a surge of stress hormones. (Mayo Clinic News Letter, 2016)

(CHAPTER 11)

She could never get a break. She was born in a family that is far from being close knit. Her mother emotionally abused her calling her "blue black, fat, ugly, and ignorant" whenever she did something even remotely incorrect. She hardly ever saw her mother since she worked 2 full-time jobs to provide for the family of 5, for which she was the sole bread winner. Her mother, Adelia was only home at night and on Sundays.

Her father, Lewis was only physically present when he wasn't out getting drunk with his friends. When he was home, Lola was completely ignored since he would be nodding and always sleeping off his liquor; and she knew she had better not disturb him or she would get a thrashing with his old, cracked, thick, brown leather belt. Her other 2 siblings, Delilah and Daphne were of a much lighter hue and seemed to get more attention and better treatment from the family. They were, "Dad's P.Y.T.'s" (pretty young things), as he would affectionately refer to them.

This hurt Lola deeply, and she would sit in the closet of the room she shared with her siblings and cry for hours with no one even noticing she was missing. This went on for years, and she eventually approached age 13. Her paternal uncle, Milton, would come by often since he really didn't have much else to do with his life other than visit the family, have a few drinks and watch cable. His brother, Lewis, would awake occasionally, mumble a few words and nod back off when he was over visiting.

The 2 younger sisters, Daphne and Delilah were ages 10 and 11; not only were they were very close in age, also in their relationship. They always played together in the backyard, leaving Lola out. They were impressionable and bought into the treatment their sister received from the rest of the family. They didn't want to include her in any games they played, but Lola eventually learned to mentally block out the treatment and lived as if she were the only child. Her uncle noticed her loneliness and physical maturity.

He began touching her inappropriately, which eventually escalated to penetration. He would get away with it since he knew his brother was always in a deep drunken sleep, his sister- in-law was hardly ever home, and the 2 younger girls were always off in their own world together in the backyard or in their bedroom with the door closed playing one of their myriad of games. This molestation went on until Lola was 16 before she finally told her parents. Neither of them believed her and Milton denied it claiming, "She just wants attention and don't care how she gets it".

Lola's broken life led her to flee from home at age 17 with no idea how she would make it, but she never looked back. She ended up with a few guys over the next few years who allowed her to reside with them - for a price of course. The first one used her as his own personal sex machine, requiring he had access to her 2-3 times per day. After she finally left him, she moved in with another guy who would physically harm her whenever he lost his temper, which was quite often. Lola would be forced to walk around with a bloody nose from him smacking her across her face, bruises on her arms and legs from his punches and a sore scalp from him yanking her by the hair.

When she had enough of the beatings and left, she stayed at a few homeless shelters and ended up trying marijuana, then begin mixing the marijuana with powder cocaine, and eventually escalated to full blown crack-cocaine. She ultimately commenced to running the streets with drug addicts for a couple of years. She figured out she was pregnant when she stopped menstruating, but had no means or the knowledge of what resources were available to her for prenatal care and/or other assistance.

She then met a guy named Sid who had what Lola perceived as financial stability from his monthly disability stipend due to his declining mental instability, which also caused him to be medically discharged from the Military's Counter-Intelligence Unit several years prior. He took an interest in Lola despite her looking to be about 8 months pregnant and allowed her to move in with him. Sid also indulged in snorting and smoking cocaine occasionally just as Lola. She felt she would finally be able to leave her life of bouncing from shelter to shelter, couch to couch, and man to man. They had their occasional arguments and he came with a few idiosyncrasies, but according to her, things were fine.

By this time she was 9 months pregnant, but still getting high occasionally with her new beau. She felt so secure since she finally had the stability she longed for after living pillar to post. He treated her better than she had ever been treated before in her entire life, but it was only good to her because she had only known worse and never experienced better.

He would belittle her when she didn't clean the house like he wanted it cleaned and would often throw up in her face how he made her the woman she is and often tell her, "You wouldn't' be shit if it wasn't for me!" and, "I met you with nothing and if you leave you'll leave with nothing!" But Lola thought at least he didn't beat her like her last boyfriend, call her names like her mother did, ignore her like her father and sisters did, or use her as a sex machine as her Uncle Milton and her ex did. He even provided her with clothes in addition to the shelter, food, and periodic drugs. He rarely even wanted to be intimate, which she found strange, but it was fine with her since she really never wanted to be penetrated again anyway after enduring so much sexual abuse.

She finally delivered a healthy baby girl despite the substances she used while pregnant. She named the baby Layla, after her, someone she vowed to love like she had never been loved before. She trusted Sid in spite of the emotional abuse, which was the first time she had truly trusted anyone. He showed affection to Layla that Lola never received from her father and she was proud of that.

Sid was very protective over the baby as well. However, it was actually more possessive, but Lola viewed it as overly affectionate and being over protective, something she wish she received from her father. She finally begin to feel she was getting a break from the broken life she has always known and felt her daughter can have the love from a mother and father that she deserves and that she was never fortunate enough to experience.

Lola even felt comfortable leaving the child with Sid while she went shopping or running errands for a couple of hours, although she had only met him a few months ago. Life was not the best for Lola with the constant emotional abuse, but in her opinion it was looking much better than what she was used to.

The baby was now 4 months old and a friend Lola met at one of the shelters she kept in contact with over the phone here and there was having a birthday party. She was elated to be invited since she had never experienced a party before. As she pranced and danced around the house getting prepared for the party, she told Sid not to wait up for her. He didn't mind since he had no kids of his own, had taken such an eerie liking to the baby and knew he would get to spend one on one time with her for the majority of the night. This would be the first time she would be gone away from her child for longer than 2 or 3 hours.

It was 9:00pm and she didn't plan on coming back until the wee hours of the morning. As her friend came to pick her up for the party she kissed Layla and told her beau, hasta la vista, but didn't bother kissing or hugging him since she learned he did not take too much of a liking to affection toward him when she tried to show it throughout the relationship - and off she went. It was her first party ever although she was a full grown adult since she had never even been to a kid's party before.

Lola partied the night away and had fun with all the friends she met over the past couple of years in homeless and domestic violence shelters. They caught up with each others' lives since many of them had not seen or heard from her since she left the shelter. Some of them were recently clean from their drug use, a few of them had finally had their own places, many of the other friends they were unable to contact, a couple others had also gotten into relationships and she told them how everything was fine with her and how affectionate Sid was with the baby.

They all thought it was great that he loved Layla just as she was his biological child. However, one of the friends who had been sober for several months made a comment about how she would not trust him watching her baby girl being that Lola has not even known him a for a year. Lola brushed the comment off and they continued dancing, drinking, smoking, laughing and talking.

The party was finally over; Lola had partied the night away and was dropped back off at home at approximately 4:30am. She peeked in on her daughter in her room by cracking the door to her nursery and figured she was fast asleep although she couldn't see her with all of the stuffed animals in the crib despite the night light being on, but figured since she was not making any crying or cooing sounds she was fine. She then went down the hall to her bedroom and felt her way to her side of the bed since it was too dark to see and she didn't want to turn on the bright light and disturb Sid. She took off her clothes, put on a t-shirt and shorts she had lying across the night stand from the night before and slid into bed.

As she reached over and decided to gently wake him to tell him about her night out with the girls because she was too anxious to wait until morning and to see how the night went with the baby, she noticed amongst all of the pillows strewn about the king sized bed was a wet, cool, sticky feel. She then jumped up to turn the light on and saw the bed was saturated with a bright red substance. As she begin screaming and frantically pulling the covers back and throwing the pillows off the bed there was a gruesome discovery!

She initially thought it was Sid, but he was nowhere to be found. Her baby's limp, bloody, mutilated naked body was lying in the center of the bed. Lola screams to the top of her lungs, tears streaming down her face and she calls 911 while panicking, pacing the floor, and barely being able to breathe! She eventually dropped to her knees describing hysterically to the dispatcher what she has discovered. After the ambulance rushed to the address, one of the paramedics grabbed the baby while another tries to calm Lola down as she climbs in the ambulance with her Layla.

The Paramedics try diligently to resuscitate the baby for the whole 12 minute ride to the hospital. However, she was D.O.A., Lola had no idea what happened, which is what she also told law enforcement at the hospital while still crying uncontrollably. She informed them of her coming back from a birthday party to the catastrophe. The doctor then came out and informed her of the medical findings.

The baby's vaginal walls were split open, her eyes had been shaken out of the sockets and she had gigantic bite marks, one on her inner thigh and one on her cheek that left her skin flapping off from the injuries. Her paramour had molested, shook, and bit her baby to death. The doctor stated he could not determine which of the injuries were the exact cause of death, and stated the shaken baby syndrome and the excessive bleeding were both enough to kill the child.

An intense man hunt ensued for Sid and his photograph was all over the news and social media. The following night he was found by the U. S. Marshalls hiding out in an abandoned building not to far from their home. The incident caused Lola to develop homicidal tendencies, Depression, Anxiety, along with Schizophrenia and she never was the same again. Her life was doomed for failure since birth. Her abusive upbringing led to her poor choices in life, which ultimately led to her destruction and trickled down to her child's demise.

Sid's defense was that he got high, blacked out, and had no recollection of what happened. He stated the last he remembered the baby was fine and asleep when he went out to buy a bag of crack thinking he can make it back home before she would awake, but after a few hits of the substance on his way back to the house mixed with the alcohol that was already in his system, he never made it back and had no idea how or why he ended up in the abandoned building. His story sounded ridiculous to all who heard it, but he was sticking to it.

After the autopsy, the coroner found no semen in or on the baby's body and all other DNA findings were justified since Sid resided in the same household with the child. The bite marks were from standard dentures, which could not be pinpointed to the paramour since there were thousands of the same models of dentures made and there were no distinguishing marks since the dentures were brand new. Sid was not found with any blood on his clothes and admitted he took a shower and changed before leaving the baby to go out & get high. When the detectives asked for the clothes he had on before his shower, he told them it was the green checkered pajamas in the hamper, which did not have a drop of blood, and of course Sid denied removing any evidence from the home and in his statement said it must have been an intruder since he left the back sliding glass door unlocked to avoid anyone seeing him leave out of the front door.

After a lengthy trial, the community demanding answers and a media circus surrounding the case, there was still not enough evidence to convict Sid of murder. However, he was charged with Child Neglect and Child Endangerment for leaving the baby alone in the home and served 5 years in prison. Lola thought not even her child could get a break in life. She moved away and no one she knew ever saw or heard from her again.

❖ Though all the events leading up to the end of this story are all fictional, the death of the child and short prison sentence is true; this account was told to me by someone I once counseled. R.I.P. to the young infant who suffered this brutal death in 1994 when she was just 4 months old.

THE DEPARTED
(CHAPTER 12)

Darla was an ordinary girl, she loved the typical things in life; hanging out with friends, shopping and going out to eat. She was also a nature girl and enjoyed long walks in the fall to take pleasure in the multi-colored leaves high up in the trees, and how they randomly gravitated so gently to the ground, making snow angels in the winter by day, and watching the beautiful white flakes glistening from the light of the stars from her bedroom window by night, walking through the neighborhood early spring mornings as the sun peeked over the horizon so she could enjoy the beautiful array of colorful flowers slightly hinted with dew in everyone's front yards, and splashing around with friends in cool water at the nearby lake during the hot summers.

Everyone adores Darla; she has a sweet personality and absolutely loves to have fun. They also admired her because she could eat anything no matter how many calories it contained and would never put on a single pound. She was 29 years old and still weighed only 112 pounds, which was not far from the same amount she weighed in high school.

As a free spirit, she was spontaneous, had no children, and was not tied down to any particular guy at this time. She dated here and there, but preferred socializing more with the group of friends she had known for years. However, she was always welcoming to any newcomers who were a friend of a friend.

Their favorite place to socialize together was Boulder Park; it got its name from having so many different sized and shaped boulders and rocks throughout the recreational area there. They would sometimes bring lunch, a frisbee, and a ball to just enjoy the day there together with no worries. Darla also often used the beautiful area of rocks, trails, trees, and benches when she wanted some alone time to think, especially since she lived only a 10 minute walk away.

Boulder Park was the safest place of all, no major issues had ever been reported there, only a couple of complaints of a few disobedient guys riding their mopeds through the trail, which was prohibited. Darla practically grew up in Boulder Park; her parents took her there often as a child growing up, and she continued the tradition as an adolescent and adult.

Although Darla was overall very happy, she still had inner issues she was grappling with; mainly of which direction to go in her life. She was ready to have a career, but was unsure of exactly what she wanted to do. She did not want to be stuck doing a job she hated, but knew it was time for her to make a decision, especially since her parents were starting to be on her more about what she was going to do with her life and how long did she plan on living with them. They loved Darla dearly, but knew it was time to nudge her out of the nest.

She decided to go to her favorite thinking place at the park by a huge rock she loved to sit on. She took her notepad and a pen to write down different ideas about her future, as well as the pros and cons of which career path to take. She yelled up to her mother as she was leaving out of the front door, "I'll be back mom, I'm going to the park for a bit!"

It was midday in the middle of April and slightly chilly out, but still sunny and beautiful. Darla was writing and thinking alone on her favorite boulder, she loved how it was so huge with craters throughout it - which helped her have a good grip to climb up and sit at the very top of it. The park was usually bustling with people walking, jogging, biking, or picnicking on the weekends, but was quiet and empty today since most of the populace were at work or school with only an occasional person in the distance every so often.

Night began to fall, Darla's mother began to worry that she was not back yet for dinner. She tried calling her, but the phone kept going straight to voicemail, she left several messages, but Darla did not return any of her calls, which was out of character. Darla's father told her mother not to worry and maybe the battery is dead. Mrs. Copeland reminded Mr. Copeland how Darla would have been back by now after going to the park for several hours, especially since she went alone, knew her cell phone battery was getting low and wouldn't dare be out there alone in the dark regardless of how safe it was.

At about 10:00 pm Mrs. Copeland begin calling a few of Darla's friends to see if they had heard from her, they each said no or not today or not since yesterday. When the clock struck midnight and she still was not back yet, Mrs. Copeland and her husband went to the park for themselves. Mr. Copeland grabbed a flashlight since the park is only dimly illuminated at night from the lights surrounding the city.

They walked through the park together calling out to her, "Darla! Darla! There was no response. They called the authorities who said they would have to wait until the next day to file a missing persons report since Darla was 29 years old, had been last seen earlier that day, and has the right to go missing if she wanted to. The Officer also tried to calm Mrs. Copeland by telling her, "We get these calls all the time, the person usually shows back up by the next day". It did not go well, Mrs. Copeland knew her daughter.

Disappointed and upset, the Copeland's continued calling her phone, her friends' phones, and walking through the park calling for her. It became very late, so they went home, got a little sleep - and the very next morning at daybreak, which was only a few hours after they went to bed, went right back out to the park. A few of Darla's friends went with them after concern continued to grow. There were several of them walking around the park and looking in Darla's favorite spots to see if there were any signs of her. One of her friends came across her notebook and pen, which was barely visible and embedded between a couple of the boulders, right next to the one Darla always climbed and sat on.

Mrs. Copeland used this information to contact the police again. A few squad cars were sent out to investigate. One of the detectives put the notebook and ink pen into a plastic bag and a missing persons report was filed. Darla's parents and friends went back to the house and immediately begin creating and printing missing person signs to post around the city and the park. Days turned into weeks and weeks into months. Darla was still not heard from. Family, friends, the authorities and the community were baffled as to what happened.

The detectives did their routine questioning to everyone close to Darla and others who lived nearby the park and her home. Nothing came of it. Eventually, those months turned into years and no one ever heard from Darla again. Her friends were all building careers, getting married and having children. Mr. and Mrs. Copeland now well into their 70's remained broken hearted, but still kept a glimmer of hope that did not seem to be shared by many others. Darla would now be 51 years old, but everyone remembers her as the young, happy and free spirited 29 year old she departed as.

Departed Soul

I do not know you personally
But I **still** feel your pain
You lost one of the closest people in your **world**
But their spiritual presence will remain
This is a difficult time for you
But others who care will help you maintain
They were born your loved one
And left just the same
Sometimes things happen

And cannot be explained
Remember them by the good times
And know its ok for cries
They're now the angel on your shoulder
Who'll still be there for your lows and highs
See, it was time for them to rise
Into the heavens and the skies
Where we will **all** meet again
When **our** time has arrived

Words of Wisdom:

Always build and treasure memories, one day for every single one of us, it will be all that is left of genuine meaning for our loved ones.

THE SECRET KEY

(CHAPTER 13)

They both had one around their necks in the form of a necklace. It went to a special lock that both mother and daughter only had access to, they refer to it as - the secret key. However, they did not always have to have this key. It was carved in metal after holes in their hearts were carved with pain.

Bill was a loving father and adored his daughter. She was the only child between him and his wife Jan. They both worked full time jobs and took turns picking her up from day care, then eventually grammar school. They went on family trips, visited parks and attended PTA meetings; everything that encompasses the American dream. On the outside looking in, they were the epitome of what a family should and could be. However, there lied a sinful side.

Bella, the now 8 year old daughter of Bill and Jan loved to play downstairs in the basement. It was where many of her older toys were stored, and she enjoyed revisiting the Cabbage Patch Kids, Barbie dolls, tea set, as well as various other toys she received over the years from birthdays, Christmas and just because gifts. She was the only child, had a limitless imagination and was doted on by both parents. She was in another world when going downstairs to what was considered her playroom. She had done this for the last few years after her mother was getting tired of the abundance of toys and games taking up so much space upstairs, and after several times trying to rationalize with Bella to give them away was to no avail.

Her father Bill was no help by taking the child's side stating, "They're her toys and she should decide what she wants to give away and what she wants to keep, it's not like we don't have the room for them". Jan eventually obliged and Bella reveled in her new sizeable playroom in the basement where all of the toys were moved.

Jan often worked later than Bill leaving him to pick up Bella from school most days of the week, and she preferred to do the grocery shopping after work since he seemed to always forget something or get the wrong item she wrote on the list anyway. This left him and his daughter to have more quality time together. Bill would sometimes join Bella in the playroom for fun and games. She loved this time with her father. Her favorite games with him were tea parties - where her dad would allow her to use real tea when he played along with her; and house, where they played with the dolls, cooked on the plastic stove, used the Easy Bake Oven and washed the toy dishes in the miniature sink that allowed for real bubbles and water.

However, Bella's extensive imagination was sometimes crossed with a confusing reality. Her dad would tell her he is playing husband and would touch her inappropriately telling her she is the wife when they played house. He told her not to tell mommy about the husband and wife game, only the other games because she may get really mad and give all of the toys away. Bella did not want this to happen, so she obeyed her father's request. This went on for years, even as Bella became too mature to be interested in playing house any longer.

Her dad had advanced to more than just touching by this time and would still have his way with her in her bedroom after his wife was fast asleep. Bella kept this secret from her mother Jan, as well as everyone else all of this time and she was in middle school now.

One night Bill got up to make his way to his daughter's bedroom after his wife fell asleep, which was his routine 1-2 nights per week; this night it was thundering and lightening pretty bad due to a heavy storm that was passing through. Jan who was a heavy sleeper, usually slept even better when it was raining out, however this particular night a lightning bolt came down so bright and loud that Jan hastily awakened from her sleep. She looked over to see that her husband was not in bed, she thought he was in the bathroom or the kitchen grabbing a drink of water, but after 15 minutes and he still was not back in bed, she slid on her slippers and went to find out where he was.

As she quietly walked through the house taking a look in each room, she begin to worry as room after room there was no sign of Bill. She looked out the window to see if his car was in the driveway, it was. She then went to Bella's room to make sure she was OK, to her horrific surprise she saw Bill lying behind Bella, both of them under the covers while Bill was gyrating. She turned on the light and loudly screamed - BILL, WHAT THE HELL ARE YOU DOING??!!

Bill jumped out of the bed stuttering and staggering while stating he was trying to help Bella get back to sleep after the loud storm awakened her. Jan then looked at Bella and said Bella, what was your father doing. Bella just begin to cry and ran into her mother's arms. As they embraced, Bill walked out of the room with his face as red as a beet and his forehead and chest so sweaty it looked as if he had just came in from being outside in the rain storm. Jan slammed the door closed, turned on the television to block out the sound of their conversation and begin comforting and probing Bella about what just transpired.

Bella opened up to her mother saying to her, "I never felt right all of the times it was happening, I was so scared to say anything since dad told me if you ever found out I would have to be put in a foster home with new parents". Bella stated she was terrified of being taken away and never told anyone. Jan then asked Bella how long this had been going on, Bella told her mother it all started when she and her father would play house in the basement together where he would be the husband and she would be the wife. Jan paused, thought back for a moment and stated, "You were only 8 years old when we moved your toys into the basement".

She then let out a screeching cry and held Bella tighter. She slept in the room with Bella for the remainder of that night consoling her. The next morning, she dropped Bella off at middle school and told her to not say anything to anyone at school about this, that they would handle it as a family and that she would be the only one picking her up and dropping her off at school from this point forward. Bella agreed.

Bill was not home when they left nor was he home when they came back from work and school. Jan had 2 locks installed on Bella's bedroom door, an inner and an outer lock. Both locks took the same key; Jan had a key made for her and one for Bella that they wore around their necks to enter and exit from Bella's room, Bella was instructed by her mother to never remove the necklace or the key and neither would she.

Bill would no longer have access to Bella at night nor during the day since Jan also changed her work hours. Bill returned home after being gone for 5-6 days. Jan, Bella, or Bill never said a word about the incident again. Life went on; Bella graduated high school and left home. Bill and Jan remained estranged together in the family home. They continued to attempt to put on airs to outsiders of a perfect family home, while allowing that incident to go on unaddressed and buried. The secret key remained the family secret.

Words to Remember:

❖ We never know what's going on behind closed doors and what type of past people are presently living with. Sometimes those who seem the most perfect, can be the most flawed.

VAGICIDAL

(CHAPTER 14)

Isn't she lovely? She was born a beautiful baby girl in the middle of summer, and that's what she was named, Summer. She grew up to be as sweet as pie to anyone who came her way. She loved meeting new like-minded people, indulging in new experiences and having stimulating conversations. She always played with others as a child and was a social butterfly as a teen, even with the ones others deemed as weird or different.

She eventually met a guy one day when she was just the tender age of 14, he was 4 years her senior. Many members of both of their adult families disapproved of the relationship due to the age difference; however, it was the beginning of a blossoming teen romance.

Her father had not been in the picture since she was elementary school age, which left her with no positive male guidance or protection. At age 16 she and her first love had their first child; she adored that baby boy and eventually dropped out of school to care for him full time. The child's father over time became very violent and addicted to drugs compelling her to move on for her safety, as well as her offspring's. A year later, she enrolled in a night school program to obtain the high school diploma she once left behind.

During that time, she met another guy. She didn't find him very attractive and he wasn't her type, but he was funny, walked her home from school every night like the perfect gentlemen and was persistent in his pursuit of her, so she eventually gave in. They became an item and he introduced her to his family. She fit right in, his family became her family and a year later she was pregnant with her second baby at age 18. Unfortunately, she miscarried after being 4 months pregnant due to the stress of learning her man was also in another relationship with someone else simultaneously that also was pregnant with his child.

This hurt her more than she had ever been hurt before. The mental anguish pierced her harder and lasted longer than the physical abuse from her previous relationship. She was not close with her mother and had no other wise mature female adult to confide in throughout the ordeal. She eventually forgave him, they tried the relationship again, she conceived and they soon gave birth to a healthy baby girl.

His family was great and even treated her first born like he was their biological grandchild. The young couple eventually moved into their own place together, but a couple of years after, she asked him to leave since he could never find the time to be home with her and the children due to his busy lifestyle of hanging out with the fellows after work every day and frequent weekend visits to the strip clubs.

As a single parent with 2 children to take care of now, she eventually regained her focus, enrolled in college, obtained a full time job while his parents continued to be instrumental and helped with childcare as she endured years of working various jobs and intense studying. In the process, she met a handsome successful business owner who was impressed with her ambition, resilience, intelligence, and complimented her on how she had the whole package of beauty, personality and brains, which he found hard to find and to resist; however, after the second date, he learned she had 2 children and was no longer interested, stating he was "not ready for a ready-made family". Saddened, she respected his decision, thanked him for his honesty and kept it moving.

Thereafter, she met a nice-looking "street pharmacist". It was instant attraction; he took good care of her and provided her with the finest of everything - vacations, 5 star restaurants, shopping sprees, multiple cars to drive, even helping her pay her way through college. However, 4 ½ years later it all came crashing down when he was sentenced to a long prison term for one of his various street crimes. She was deeply hurt by the absence of her man, but in the recesses of her mind knew that it was probably best since she was beginning to endure domestic violence and he was hardly ever home due to his paper chase and who knows what else he was chasing.

Eight months later, when she was able to mentally move on, she came in contact with a good-looking lightly hued brother who came to the electric company to pay his bill where she was employed as a Clerk. He sent her flowers to the job, spent quality time with her, took her on nice dates and allowed her to drive his expensive car. He then says the "L" word, "I love you". Finally! She screams mentally. She thinks she eventually has the long-term true love she has dreamed of all her life. At last, love, something she felt she never genuinely received from her father or her mother. Conversely, he turns out to be a master manipulator. After their first intimate encounter several months into the relationship, he dropped off the face of the earth. Refusing to answer or return any of her calls. She is crushed, but like every other time, moves on.

A year later she meets a different promising potential paramour; but he made it crystal clear in the beginning that he was not interested in a relationship, only a "special friend". She goes along with it hoping it will flourish into what she truly desires. After 6 months, she realizes he refuses to budge from the original arrangement and has to cut him loose. She feels dejected, lonely, and confused trying to figure out what is she doing wrong.

Summer eventually graduates from the university and she and the kids move out of the state for a fresh new start. It is a little bumpy initially, but exciting and things eventually smooth out. She meets a striking guy who has no ambition, but treats her well giving her foot massages after a long day at work, starting dinner when he gets off from his job, and is a very well-mannered gentleman to her and an awesome step-father to the kids. It lasts a few years, but she eventually had to part ways with him since he prefers congregating more with his brothers and their friends playing video games and smoking ganja all weekend; additionally, his lack of ambition is totally swallowed by hers, she was well out of his league, she knew it and decided to give it a chance anyway, a decision she did not regret since she always lived by the mantra, "You'll never know if you never try".

She then runs into a guy 7 years her junior. She's skeptical at first due to the age difference, but relents after an extensive dialogue reveals his advanced maturity level, intelligence, chivalry, and ample ambition, which was matched by hers. The relationship was beautiful, and they became engaged, but as all of the other experiences, begins to cave in when she sees that his baby mama drama, past drug felony that was hindering him from obtaining a better career and child support debt was taking over his life, not to mention, he started taking out his frustrations on her.

He even displays anger management issues and wraps his hands around her neck during a few heated arguments towards the end of their relationship on more than one occasion. She returns his engagement ring and partially moves on. Yes, partially. They linger for a couple of months after he moves out trying to see if the relationship can be salvaged. She hates to let go, but realizes it is the best solution since nothing seemed to be improving.

Summer finds herself back to square one, a single working parent with no ideal significant other, not to mention with no help from her children's 2 fathers. Nevertheless, she continues to progress in school and with life, consistently bettering herself and vacationing here and there with female friends or an occasional nice well-to-do guy, but still longs for that one true love who comes without so much baggage, who is not too far from her level with morals, dreams, character, ambition and who can financially hold his own with street smarts, as well as the ability to maneuver through the corporate world, start a business or the resourcefulness to generate a decent legit income.

To her it seems impossible to meet such a mate. The men who are financially stable want to be players, thinks the females should pursue them, or are mentally unstable and the ones who are still living with their mothers and/or under employed and have little or nothing to offer are the ones who want a relationship. All of her female friends tell the same accounts of their experiences, the ones who live out west, up north and in the south. She feels despair and thinks she will just have to face her reality; the good men are not available, the available men are not good, the others are locked up for good or looking for the same goods… as they have.

The random guys she continue to meet and date here and there are mostly interested in sex, expects the woman to trade places to take on the male's leadership role, can't converse intelligently about any subject, don't have themselves together, or are just too closed minded.

This trend continues until her children reach adulthood and move out on their own. Her years of sacrifice, ambition, and hard work have afforded her the almost perfect life now. Summer is able to live in an upscale neighborhood equipped with immaculately manicured lawns, a pool, tennis court, purchase a brand new sports car off the showroom floor, dresses to kill with a mean shoe game, and has a decent sized bank account; however, she is still missing one key element, the love of her life.

She is getting fed up with a life of heartache and headache from men, memories of being played, physically abused as well as ignored by those who prefer the low hanging fruit and have no desire to put in the effort to climb to the top of the tree, and she can no longer take it. She starts beginning to feel as if she has nothing to live for and deals with it by putting on some soulful R&B music, lights several fragranced candles and pour rose petals all over the heated bedroom and marble bathroom floors. She slides into the garden tub filled with nice hot steamy bubbly water, soaks, thinks, and relaxes for a bit. She then reaches over to grab her pen and paper and begins writing a heartfelt poem she entitles, "Mentally Mangled by Men":

There was once this older girl

And up to this point, she had various **guys** in her world

She thought each would treat her right

But no not quite

They gave her much strife

Throughout her young adult life

The 1st cheated, the 2cnd hit her

The 3rd tried to **get** with her **friend**

The 4th, after he hit it

He never **called** her again

The one after that

Played so many games

He slipped **up** a few times and called her somebody **else's**

name

The last one would look her directly in the **eyes**

And tell her artificial **lies**

She was tired of the **jive** so she **cocked** a 45

Not to harm them, was what she'd decide

She put the gun between her **thighs** and blew out her **own**

insides

However. She did survive

And figured, she'd never be used for sex again

Even if they tried

She was physically **OK**

But had **mentally died**

   After the long comforting bubble bath and cathartic
poem, she pulls herself out of the garden tub and grabs her
pink pearl and chrome plated pistol she had locked away

for years that she is thankful she never had to use on anyone, inserts the barrel inside her vagina and pulls the trigger, (click, click, POW!).

Yes, Summer decided to off herself from below as a symbol of her feeling used and abused after she had given her heart, soul, and loving to these men in her life who would never do right by her. She was "vagicidal". Fortunately, Summer survived the attempted vaginal suicide incident and had plenty of time to contemplate while she was in bed for several weeks recovering. She learned a valuable lesson, that it was not her turn or time to cross over and exit the universe and that the one thing she could have and should have done was recognize the flags of all of the men in her past before allowing herself to fall for them and have to endure painful relationship breakups that were all bound for failure before they even began.

Allowing the street pharmacist, the guy with no ambition, the man with the baby mama drama and drowning child support debt, falling for someone's words and superficial actions were all mistakes that could have prevented the inevitable heartache she endured over the years. Lessons she had to learn all the hard way. Summer now travels to different universities, community centers, and high schools telling her story and speaking to young women about waiting, taking their time to learn someone before jumping into a relationship, using protection, flags to be aware of, how to not settle for someone who is not on their level, how to take advantage of their time while being single by enjoying and living life to the fullest, how precious life is, and how to never attempt a permanent solution to a temporary problem.

She receives thousands of Direct Messages, letters, and emails annually from young girls and women around the world thanking her for her insight, advice, and for sharing her horrific experience, as well as showing their gratitude for how she helped prevent them from getting into toxic relationships or motivated them to get out of the relationships they were currently in that were predestined for failure.

Words of Wisdom:

If you live through something that could have taken you away; recognize your purpose and start sharing it today.

WHITE HURRICANE

(CHAPTER 15)

Everything was going great. He graduated high school, went to college and obtained a degree as a Chemical Engineer. He and his girlfriend discussed her dropping out of college when she discovered she was pregnant with their first child. He promised her if she would just be a full time mother he would take good care of her and the baby and explained to her how he was not comfortable with his child being in daycare around well-meaning strangers all day everyday with so much going on in the world these days, she agreed. Rich promised her once the child was old enough to enroll in school, he would pay for her to complete her college degree, so she accommodated his request.

It was all Rich ever wanted, a nice career and a loving family. He fulfilled his promise and took great care of the family. They married, he purchased a comfortable home in a nice quiet upper-middle class area and took the family on a national and international vacation every year. Victoria, his wife, who was also his college sweetheart, stayed busy going to the gym daily where an open "Kiddie Area" was available for parents to look after their children while they get a nice sweaty work out in, and she also arranged play dates with other stay-at-home moms from the neighborhood at parks, at each other's homes, or other kid friendly locations.

Victoria was enjoying her new family life and loved that she was fortunate enough to stay home with her child to be a full time mother until he became school aged. Then there was a pleasant surprise; Victoria thought she was pregnant again, but was not sure so she did not say anything to Rich about it yet. However, it was confirmed at her OB/GYN visit, that she was going to conceive baby number 2! She was delighted and could not wait to break the news to Rich. She decided to surprise him by having pink balloons floating around the house when he got home from work that read, "It's a girl!"

When Rich came home he thought Victoria was throwing a Baby Shower that she didn't tell him about for one of her friends. He asked her, "Which one of your friends is the lucky lady?" Victoria happily and bashfully responded, you're looking at her. Rich did a double take and said, "You're the pregnant one?!" Victoria smiled and said yes. Rich scooped her up off her feet, gave her a huge hug and kiss and said, "That's wonderful baby! I can't wait to share the news; Ricky is going to have an adorable little sister to care for and we are going to have an addition to the family".

Victoria still wanted to go back to college eventually, but realized things don't always go as planned and was happy she was pregnant now so that the children would be close in age. By having another child at this time, both children could be in school before she went back to finish her degree. She and Rich decided 2 children were all they needed.

Life continued to go on with annual family vacations, play dates, friendships with other stay- at-home moms in the neighborhood, socializing with other married couples with children, dropping the kids off with family so they can have romantic dates sometimes, etc. The only thing that changed was the way they vacationed. This year Rich decided the family would go on a road trip for their next getaway. Victoria was elated and thought that would be a fantastic idea and something different since they usually always flew to their destinations. Rich rented a mini RV for 2 weeks for the trip. They decided they would drive from Michigan to Florida to enjoy the everlasting summer temperatures there before the Michigan winter arrived.

Rich and Victoria packed their bags, grabbed the babies, and excitedly hopped in the RV headed south towards the beaches and palm trees. By this time Ricky was 2 years old and Stormy, a name they gave their daughter because it was a heavy down pour of rain, blustery wind and lightning when she was born, was now 6 months old. It was October, Rich knew since the snow typically did not fall until November or December, if they headed out early October, they would be back well before snowfall to avoid having to drive the family in the RV on slippery roads leaving or coming back.

Off to Florida they went, it was a 3 day drive since they stopped to sight see in different cities they passed through and parked the RV to rest a few times prior to arriving to their destination in the Sunshine State. They had one of the best times of their life. They got a chance to see Florida's beautiful oceans, experience the non-stop waves, collected seashells at the beach, purchased souvenir tee shirts for themselves and the children, and bought magnets as well as key chains to give out to friends and family members when they returned home.

They ate at ocean front seafood restaurants and tried conch and oysters for the first time. They enjoyed them and said they would seek out places that served them when they get back to Michigan. Victoria even pulled a few seafood restaurants up on her cell phone to visit when they returned home. They decided at that moment to start exploring their palates a lot more when they traveled, as well as when they returned home instead of just sticking to the basics.

The trip finally came to an end. It was time to pack up and go; they all had sun-kissed skin and took countless pictures and videos of memories that would last a lifetime. They could not wait to get back home to share their experience of the road trip with their family and friends. As they were driving up Interstate 75 heading home, they were finally back in Michigan and had just a few hours travel time left to arrive at the family home.

However, things did not go according to plan. Although Rich planned to beat the snow by nearly a month's time, Mother Nature had other intentions. They ran into a blizzard that came outside of the usual snow season, about a month earlier than normal, putting a damper on the family's plan to make it home in plenty of time before what they thought would be the first snowfall.

Rich decided to just drive slowly for the last 3 hours which he knew would turn into 9 hours by only driving 20 MPH in the snow. He did this for about 60 minutes and the weather became so inclement, he could no longer see out of the windshield even with the wipers on top speed and the defroster on full blast. This forced him to pull over on the side of the expressway under an overpass with his hazards on and headlights still beaming until the blizzard let up some.

They had the radio on the weather station and the Meteorologist was stating how major snowstorms and the month of October typically do not commingle, and how the month usually brings cool, clear nights, with only the first frost of the season. The Weather Forecaster continued to explain how the current snowstorm is being very destructive, weighing down tree branches and power lines, causing them to break from the weight of the snow in addition to gusty winds blowing the snow-covered trees and power lines violently around, potentially leading to a very damaging and dangerous situation. The media nicknamed the snow blizzard, "White Hurricane".

While they continued to wait on the side of the road for the snow to let up, a few other cars and trucks slowly passed by. However, even more vehicles were pulling over up and down the expressway as well. As they sat there trying to make the best out of the situation reminiscing about the trip; all of a sudden, out of nowhere the RV received a colossal impact! It slammed into the side of the concrete underpass and was crumpled like a balled up piece of aluminum foil in a matter of seconds.

Another vehicle who was pulled over heard the impact although he could barely see exactly what happened because of the heavy thick bright snow and low visibility. He quickly called 911 to explain that he heard a loud booming sound and think there was an auto accident about ¾ of a mile down from him since he was also seeing what appeared to be a thick black smoke searing through the snow where a van or an RV he bypassed was pulled over under the overpass.

An ambulance, police cars, and fire trucks arrived after the man gave the last exit and mile marker he remembered seeing before he pulled over. An 18 wheeler had struck the Recreational Vehicle. The truck driver was disoriented walking in circles and shivering as the officers and paramedics approached repeatedly saying, "I did not see them, I didn't mean to do it, are they going to be ok?!" The firemen had to use a hydraulic rescue tool to perform a vehicular extrication in order to cut the RV from around the family since their means of exit was impossible.

The police put the truck driver in their back seat so he could calm down, explain what happened, and to see if he was under the influence of any substances. The family was rushed to the Emergency Room and the medical staff tried their best to save the lives of the remaining survivors. The baby and toddler were dead on arrival, the mother was also unable to be saved and the father survived with severe injuries. Rich was in intensive care for 2 1/2 months before being able to go home. Almost every bone in his body was broken, but amazingly no major organs were damaged.

Rich's mother moved in to help take care of him until he was able to get back on his feet. He experienced survivor's remorse and even became suicidal. A year went past before he was able to walk again. Rich's entire personality changed. He never went back to work although his employer wanted him to return; he stopped caring about himself and others. He refused to go to therapy or the support groups the medical staff suggested. He became increasingly angry due to the loss of his entire family. He began drinking heavily and using drugs, which was something he had never done before. He eventually asked his mother to leave, lost his home and vehicle and moved into a tent in the woods with other homeless people.

Rich refused to get close with anyone and tried to emotionally distance himself from all of his family and friends so that he would not feel love anymore. He did not want to ever experience the pain of losing someone close to him again. His family was so worried about him, but realized it was what Rich wanted for now, was forced to respect his decision, and hoped that he would one day come back around.

Words of Wisdom: Don't be so quick to judge someone because of their current circumstances; you never know where they have been, what they have been through, or who they have lost to cause them to be where they are.

THE END

I can be reached for questions and/or comments at
latreseprince@mail.com

A Prince Poetry Production